Living Behind Time

a novel

also by

J.B. Hogan

Tin Hollow

Fallen: A Short Story Collection

The Rubicon: Poetry & Short Fiction

Angels in the Ozarks

The Apostate

Mexican Skies

Losing Cotton

Living Behind Time

a novel

J.B. Hogan

TIREE
PRESS

an imprint of
OGHMA CREATIVE MEDIA

OGHMA

CREATIVE MEDIA

Tiree Press
An imprint of Oghma Creative Media, Inc.
2401 Beth Lane, Bentonville, Arkansas 72712

Library of Congress Cataloging-in-Publication Data

Names: Hogan, J.B., author.
Title: Living Behind Time/J.B. Hogan |
Description: Second Edition. | Bentonville: Tiree, 2019.
Identifiers: LCCN: | ISBN: 978-1-63373-501-9 (hardcover) |
ISBN: 978-1-63373-502-6 (trade paperback) | ISBN: 978-1-63373-026-7 (eBook)
Subjects: BISAC: FICTION/Literary | FICTION/Friendship |
FICTION/Adaptations & Pastiche
LC record available at: https://lccn.loc.gov/

Tiree Press trade paperback edition August, 2019

Jacket & Interior Design by Casey W. Cowan
Editing by Gil Miller

Thanks to Casey Cowan for this incredible book cover and layout and to Gordon Bonnet for his highly skilled and professional editing.

Living Behind Time

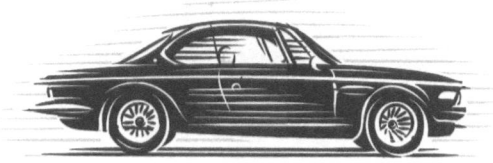

a novel

1

IT GOT HOTTER AND HOTTER as Frank Mason dropped down out of the mountains from San Diego, past Plaster City, on into the smoldering Imperial Valley. Downhill, he kept the Toyota between sixty and sixty-five, leaving the air conditioning off to keep the engine from overheating.

He loved driving through the desert in the summer. He wasn't sure why, but it was a good thing he did, because there was going to be plenty of it. Beyond the Imperial Valley was Yuma, then another two hundred and fifty miles to Tucson. After that was more desert. And after that, he wasn't sure just yet.

With the wind blasting the side of his face, he dismissed the trip that lay before him and tried to remember living here in the valley. Here among the glaring sand, the cotton and lettuce fields, the scorched adobe transient worker shacks. The heat like an oven always hitting you right at nose level. He found he couldn't imagine anyone living here. Reaching into a small cooler on the seat beside him, he extracted a chilled, nearly empty bottle of grape juice. He took a quick swig, put the bottle between his legs, and cranked the radio up a notch to better hear the nasal whine of George Jones singing about lost love.

"Eight miles to El Centro." He downed the rest of the juice and pitched the bottle into a paper sack on the floorboard.

Despite the overpowering heat, the farther he got from San Diego, the better he felt. Each mile snapped another link in the chain that bound him there. He felt the first sensations of freedom, of incipient peace of mind— happiness would be way too much to expect. He knew better than that.

It was too long, too long since he'd made a clean break from anywhere, anything. He instinctively distrusted emotional highs. Depression was the flip side of elation, and the swings between the two were often quicker, more powerful than he could comfortably manage. He drove on, feeling fine, but cautious, alert for signs of the unwanted but unsurprising reverse side to land.

"Don't whine. There's nothing or nobody to blame but yourself. You made the choices. Live with them."

He smiled self-consciously into the rear view mirror.

"Idiot." He raised the window a little to block out some of the searing wind. "You think too much."

Letting his abstract ramblings give way to a concrete need for gasoline— leaving San Diego as he had, he'd forgotten to fill the tank up—he swerved the Toyota off I-8 onto the first El Centro exit. Highway 86 North. Imperial, Brawley. It must be a hundred and fifteen in the shade.

Dust whirled across the bubbling asphalt lot of the self-service station. The sky was deep blue, but hazy. What baseball players call a high sky. For an instant he missed the cool breeze of Pacific Beach, the green shade of rich La Jolla. Just for an instant. With a swipe at the sweat trickling down his forehead, he let San Diego go.

"Twelve seventy-five on Number Two there."

"Anything else we can do for you?" The toothy station attendant kid appeared all of seventeen, maybe.

"No." Frank eyed a pack of Marlboros.

For some reason the cigarettes appealed to him just then. He tried to force himself to remember the coughing, the burning chest pain—the reasons why he'd quit in the first place. You always get those urges no matter how long after you give something up. He knew about giving things up. He'd done a lot of that in the last ten years or so. San Diego was merely the latest thing to go.

"Marlboros."

"Soft or box?"

"Box."

"Fourteen ninety-five all together."

With a whistle, he handed the attendant a ten and a five.

"Shoots that all to hell, don't it?" The attendant gave him the nickel change.

"Right."

"Going to San Diego?"

"Uh, no. . . no, just came."

"Plenty hot here, huh?"

"Yeah, plenty."

"Well, have a nice day, sir."

"Uhmp." He waved his right index finger in goodbye.

Walking back to the car, he squinted into the heat waves rising from the asphalt to see a woman emerge from behind a road sign at the curb and head toward him. He picked up his pace.

"Sir." She cut him off by the right fender. "Sir, excuse me."

He hated to be called sir. By anybody. It reminded him of the service and of his age. He didn't like to think of either.

"Yes." He checked her out. Light maroon peasant skirt over black body tights. Breasts full and firm through the thin material. No makeup and nice looking enough. Maybe in her early twenties.

"Excuse me, can I ask which way you are going?"

"I was sorta heading east."

"Oh, please. I have friends that'll pay for the gas."

"Friends?"

"Sure, they're expecting me. They'll be glad to help with the gas."

"Where, where you going?"

"Indio, I'm supposed to meet my friends there."

"How did you get here to El Centro?"

"A ride. Some insurance guy. He was a hassle. Tried to touch me all the time. He dumped me here. I've been here for hours. Couldn't you give me a ride, mister? Please."

"I don't want no hassles, either."

"I won't be trouble to you, really. All I want is a ride. It would be really wonderful of you."

"I was kind of going to Arizona."

She gave him a down and out look. He felt a twinge in the groin.

"Oh, what the hell. I'm in no hurry to get anywhere."

He climbed into the Toyota, pitched the Marlboros on the dash, moved the cooler and trash sack to the back seat, and opened the rider's side for the girl. She ran to get in, pulling the door shut after her. He took his gaze off her breasts and started the engine. Still a bit apprehensive, he pulled out of the station and headed north on Highway 86. They drove all the way through El Centro without talking.

"What do you do?" They passed the city limits sign on the way north to Imperial. She extracted a handkerchief from her large canvas bag purse and mopped the sweat off the back of her neck.

"Nothing."

"Nothing? I would have never guessed that. You look so distinguished."

He glanced at his thinning gray hair in the mirror and scratched his beard.

"I would have thought you were a businessman or a professor. Something like that."

"Something like that. But was. Past tense."

"Maybe you don't want to talk about it?"

"Oh, no, it's okay. I just lately dropped out, that's all."

"Can I have one of your cigarettes?" She pointed to the box of Marlboros.

"Sure. Help yourself."

"Want one?"

"No, I don't smoke."

"Why do you have a pack of cigarettes then?"

"I don't know. A weird impulse, I suppose."

"You don't mind if I do?" She opened the pack and took out a cigarette.

"No. But a young girl like you shouldn't smoke. Let stupid old men do it and die."

"I bet that you smoke hemp though, huh?"

"Hemp. Haven't heard that one in a while."

The girl lit her cigarette with the car lighter, neatly knocking some paper and tobacco residue into the seldom used ashtray.

"Yes, I smoke hemp. For longer than you've probably been alive."

"You're not that old."

"Damn near it." The girl wiped the back of her neck again. "Sorry it's so hot. The air conditioner does work, but I never use it in the desert on long trips. Afraid of overheating."

"That's all right." She blew smoke out the window. "I don't mind. But I do want to know what you did do. That's a fair trade, isn't it?"

"I've been a bunch of things. Mostly in computers over the past ten years or so." He wanted to pull that little bit of information back in as soon as he said it, but it didn't seem to phase the girl.

"Really, that must be interesting."

"Hardly."

When he saw the Brawley city limit sign, he considered telling the girl he'd changed his mind, Indio was at least 80 miles out of his way, but he didn't.

"You know, I used to live around here."

"In this poor little burnt-out place?"

"Yep. It was a long time ago."

"Here in this town?"

"No, the next one. And actually the one after that, too."

"I can't imagine anyone living here. I bet you must've been really bored."

"Not really. It was a different time then, you know."

"Right."

"And, besides, we had the Salton Sea and the sand dunes."

"Sand dunes?" He acted like he didn't notice her size him up in profile.

"Well, they're called sand *hills*, but they're sand dunes to me. Long time ago they made a couple of movies out there. Legend has it that some crazy dudes tried to haul a big ship, a schooner or something, across there in the 1800s sometime."

"What happened?"

"They didn't make it. Supposedly the remains are exposed now and then by the sand shifting around so much. Exotic story. Probably untrue."

"Will we go by them?"

"Not right by them, but you'll be able to see them from a distance."

"Could we go to them? I mean just for a while?"

"We'll have to walk a ways. The car'd get stuck in the sand."

"Oh, let's do. Please?"

"It will be hot. Extremely hot."

2

IMPERIAL VALLEY, CALIFORNIA—1961

THE IMPERIAL VALLEY AT THE beginning of summer was as different from the Ozarks as you can possibly imagine. Instead of rolling hills covered in beautiful green trees, there were long, flat vistas of low desert scrub and sand. Instead of building heat and humidity, there were oven-like temperatures, dry and sweat-absorbing. Frank immediately loved his new world.

Outside his little hometown in the north of the Valley, huge sand dunes ran east of the city limits some forty miles, north to south. Beyond the dunes, in the distance to the north and east were the dark, rocky Chocolate Mountains—some twenty miles away but in the pristine air of the Valley, appearing to be within arm's reach.

On an early Saturday morning, soon after his arrival, Frank's Uncle Alvin took him out to the dunes. Light brown sand, rising up in tall, long waves, beckoned. Frank leaped from his uncle's Jeep and ran down the dune on which they'd stopped. With a whoop and a yell, Frank scurried through the sand, rushing down, then starting up the next dune beyond. It was only ten a.m. but the temperature was pushing one hundred already and Frank had no idea what desert heat was lik—nor how tall the dunes really were.

"Better go easy," Uncle Alvin called out. Frank just waved and kept running.

He started up the next dune, jogging like he was running the bases in a ball game. About a quarter of the way up the dune, the deep sand began to exact its toll. Frank's pace slowed. He began to labor. Halfway up, he was barely moving and by three-quarters of the way, he was done. Completely out of breath and energy. Easily beaten by the desert sun and the sand that made his legs feel like they were made of sticks instead of bone and flesh.

He stopped in his ascent to breath and rest. Across the way, Uncle Alvin clicked a photo of Frank. Frank panted and puffed, trying to catch his breath and regain the energy needed to get to the top of the big dune.

Uncle Alvin waved at him and shouted something out but Frank couldn't hear him for his own loud breathing.

"Wh…at," came out his joked reply.

Uncle Alvin waved again and pointed at something in his hand. Frank couldn't tell what it was. He turned to look up at the top of the dune. There was no way he could make it up the rest of the way.

When he had caught his breath finally, Frank retraced his steps—easily seen in the sand—but did so at a much slower pace. He could feel his heart still pounding and he had a little bit of a headache from the exertion. Maybe he's underestimated how tall the dunes were and how hard it was to run in the sand.

"Not so easy running in the sand, is it?" Uncle Alvin laughed when Frank at last made it back to the Jeep.

"That dune was way taller than I thought it was, Uncle Alvin," Frank said, still not having fully caught his breath. Uncle Alvin laughed.

"Lot different than back home, huh?"

"Sure is."

"You'll get used to it," Uncle Alvin assured Frank. "It's a dry heat."

"Sure is hot," Frank allowed.

"Will get a lot hotter soon," Uncle Alvin laughed.

"What were you holding up for me to see when I was on the dune, Uncle Alvin?" Frank asked, when he was about breathing normally again.

"This," Uncle Alvin said, holding up a small camera. "But I imagine you'll look pretty small on that dune when we get the film developed."

"I bet," Frank said.

"Next weekend we'll go fishing on the Salton Sea" Uncle Alvin said, tossing the little camera in the back of the Jeep, "if you want to that is."

"Heck, yeah," Frank said, finally regaining his regular breathing. "That sounds like a blast."

"I don't know about a blast," Uncle Alvin kidded, "but we should have a good time. Got big Corvina out there. Big fish. Hard to bring in."

"Sounds cool."

"We'll see when you actually hook one," Uncle Alvin smiled.

After his little jog on the dunes, Frank was happy to spend the rest of their time just riding in the Jeep. It was a lot less strenuous. And Uncle Alvin really knew how to maneuver around. Up and down the dunes, over the sides, shooting over the tops. Frank had never done anything like that in his life.

With a couple of new friends already made in his new little hometown, with his mom and family and Uncle Alvin and Aunt Jean, after just a few weeks, Frank was settling into his new life pretty well.

"I'm likin' it out here, Uncle Alvin," Frank said on their way back into town.

"Well, that's good son," Uncle Alvin replied. "We're glad to have you."

"Yeah," Frank said, shaking his head. "I think I can get used to this place just fine. It's going to be alright."

"That's the spirit, boy." Uncle Alvin cheered. "The Valley's not a bad place. You'll get used to it quick and before you know it, it'll feel just like home."

"I imagine I will," Frank said, "but how did you and Aunt Belle come to live out here in the first place?"

"Oh, that's a long story," Uncle Alvin answered.

"Was it a long time ago?"

"Well, yes it was," Uncle Alvin explained. "Me and the old woman, your Aunt Belle I mean, and my brother Bob and his wife Sally come out here right before the war, right at the end of the Great Depression."

"You left back home then and came out here? What did you all do?"

"We worked in the fields mostly. Until the war."

"What happened then?"

"We got lucky," Uncle Alvin went on, "they built an army camp on the northeast side of North Shore, that's the next little town up to the north of us. Me and Bob got jobs there that took us through most of the war."

"Wow."

"After that, it was this job and that, until I got my job at the water company. That's been steady now for some years."

"Boy," Frank commented, "I bet things were different out here then, huh?"

"I'd say. A lot of the roads were still made out of wood planks so's you could get across the desert."

"Were the canals in for the all the farm fields back then?"

"They did have some canals then, but the big one, the All-American, came in right at the beginning of the war. That's when the Valley really began to be like it is today."

"Cool."

"Well, now it's your home, too. What do you think of it so far."

"I'm likin' it."

"That's good, son. Me and the old woman hope you and your family will do alright out here."

"Thanks, Uncle Alvin," Frank said, "it's going be great out here. I'm pretty sure I'm going to like it just fine."

Nodding his head, as if he had convinced himself of the truth of his own words, Frank leaned back in the Jeep and let the hot Imperial Valley wind blow on his face and through his hair. Yes, this place would be just be fine. It would be a great new home.

3

FRANK TURNED RIGHT AT THE four-way stop that was the main intersection in his old hometown and drove east six miles to where the Coachella canal split the surrounding farm land from the un-reclaimed desert. He maneuvered the Toyota over a wooden tie bridge and parked on a rocky place under a Tamarack tree a couple of hundred yards from the base of the sand dunes. The girl tried to run up the first dune they reached, collapsing in an exhausted heap about two-thirds of the way to the top.

"It'll surprise you." He puffed, reaching her side. She, too, gasped for air. "Same thing happened to me the first time I saw the dunes. They seem inviting, but they'll kick your ass."

"They... sure ... will."

"Take deep, slow breaths. You'll be okay in a second." He turned and looked west, away from the dunes. The sun was sinking, the heat slowly dissipating. "It's going to be excellent in a little while. A terrific sunset."

When the girl caught her wind, they made their way more slowly among the dunes. The first shadows of dusk crossed the sand, and a light wind tried to cool the air as they reached the top of a tall dune. He sat down facing west. The girl plopped down beside him.

"You said you used to live out here?"

"Uh-huh. A long time ago."

"You know what would hit the spot right now?"

"What?"

"A beer. A beer would be excellent, wouldn't it?"

"Sure would."

The sun was only a few degrees above the horizon, hovering orange-red in the western sky beyond the Salton Sea.

"You know something else? I don't even know your name."

He studied her. She sat back on her haunches, knees high in the air, comfortable as if she belonged out on the dunes. In the lighting, she was very pretty.

"Frank. Frank Mason."

"I'm Terri Evans." She offered her hand. He shook it lightly. It was soft and warm, but not sweaty. Remarkable, considering the situation. "Want to smoke?" She brought a fat joint and pack of matches out of a pocket in her dress.

"Sure."

The sun now hung barely above the mountains far in the distance. Perfect timing. They smoked and sat in peace. A blue haze spread across the tranquil valley with the dying of the light.

"Oh, Jesus."

"Isn't it beautiful?" The girl rested her arm on his upper thigh. A tingle shot through his body, threatening to break his rapt communion with the sunset.

"Yeah."

She nudged against him, and he reached for her hand on his thigh. They gazed at each other for a moment, then back to the sun. It was half gone now.

"Feel the wind." She pulled their coupled hands against her body, then released his hand and stood up. With little effort she removed her skirt, leaving only the body stocking. She spread the skirt across the sand. "Here, lie here."

He stretched out beside her. They lay quietly for some time, legs touching, casually linking and unlinking them as the sun finally disappeared.

"Wasn't that beautiful?"

"Yes." He picked up the burnt out roach and pointed at the ash end. "It's gone."

"Forget it." She moved nearer.

They were quiet again, legs locked together, gazing into each other's eyes. It was getting dark, the baked desert day giving way to peaceful, restorative night in the endless cycle of the arid valley.

"Maybe, I should tell you. . . ."

"No." She put a finger to his lips. "It's okay."

"I'm really stoned." His mouth nearly brushed hers. "I'm really messed up."

"Who isn't?"

"Yeah." He held her to him. "Yeah."

They rolled over in a tight embrace, bare arms touching the warm, soft sand beyond her skirt. A comfortable breeze swept over them, signaling the true end of day. He didn't notice.

4

THERE WERE ABOUT FIFTY ASSORTED latter-day hippies, post-new wave burnouts, and refried experience seekers on the farm outside Indio in disorganized breakfast mode when Terri and Frank arrived.

"Hello, everybody." She ran from the car to one of several picnic tables around which the breakfasters ate.

"Hey, Terri." They greeted her. "Where you been? We thought you weren't coming. We thought you'd got lost." Frank stood back to one side, observing the reunion. He shifted from foot to foot and tried not to feel out of place.

"Listen... listen." Terri pointed. "This is Frank Mason. He was wonderful enough to go out of his way to give me a ride. Come on over."

He stepped forward. A tall, bushy-bearded blond boy stood and offered his hand. "Welcome to the Friends of Love. It was really cool of you to give our sister a ride. That's real love, man."

Frank coughed. He slowly unwrapped his hand from the tall youth's. "Thanks."

"I'm Ted. Wanna have some food, man? There's plenty. Friends always share, we say."

"Heh, heh. Thanks, anyway. I really should get going."

Terri came over and put her arm around his waist. "Please stay for break-fast. We'll get the gas money for you. Come on, stay."

"Yeah, we're solid for the gas." Ted affirmed. "No problem."

A brunette walked up. "Yes, and you should meet Father Alpha."

"Who's Father Alpha?"

"He's our spiritual leader." Ted cast a sideways look at the brunette.

"He founded the Friends." Terri explained. "He was part of Haight-Ashbury, too."

"Ah, sure. And he was at Woodstock, too, right?" Frank chuckled into the silent stares of the Friends. "Uh—hmph. Just kidding. A little joke."

"I thought so." Ted nodded. "A sense of humor is important."

"You'll have to meet Father Alpha. He's always glad to talk to new people."

"All the same, Terri, I think I'm going to pass on that one. I gotta get rollin'."

"Won't you stay and go with us to the Joshua Tree National Monument?" The brunette smiled demurely. "It's our annual festival."

"I was going to Tucs—" Frank was interrupted by a nearby commotion.

"Father Alpha." Several of the Friends hailed their leader.

They rushed forward to greet a man who emerged from the crowd. He wore a loose-fitting white suit over a short stocky body.

To Frank's considerable discomfort, the man walked directly up to him. "So, you're the Good Samaritan who helped our sister, Terri."

Frank took in the beatific countenance of "Father Alpha," but his attention was drawn to the two companions hanging on the leader's arms.

On his right was a beautiful earth-mother type. Tall and blonde, she combined the natural beauty of Julie Christie with the innocent sensuality of Ingrid Bergman.

As beautiful as she was, the other woman to Alpha's left captured his attention. She sported a thin mustache and a full, if ragged beard. In her work shirt and dungarees, only a close examination revealed her femininity. He couldn't take his eyes off her.

Alpha read his astonishment. "We of the Friends do not believe in the absolutes of sexual identity and preference forced on us by society. Everyone here is free to be whoever they feel themselves to be."

"Uh-huh. Right."

Terri formally introduced the group's leader. "This is Father Alpha. He founded our group."

"Yeah." Frank forced himself to look again at Alpha. "I got that."

"Welcome, welcome. We're so grateful for your kindness to one of our flock. Please join us for our morning meal, won't you?"

Frank unhooked himself from Terri's arm. "Thanks. I'm glad to meet you all, really, but I've got to get on the road. I should have left already."

"Where are you going?"

"East."

"What are you seeking?" The leader put a fleshy arm on Frank's shoulder. He tensed at the contact.

"Nothing, I'm trying to escape."

"Escape from what?" Alpha grinned and squeezed his shoulder.

Frank took a step back. A number of the Friends collected around him. He peeked longingly beyond them to the Toyota.

Alpha again put an arm on his shoulder. "We believe in love, Frank. All love."

"Uh, sure, uh-huh." He lifted Alpha's hand off his shoulder.

The leader's smiling eyes went flat, reptilian. "You misunderstand."

"I'm leaving." There seemed to be a threatening new attitude from the nearby Friends.

"Stay." Alpha's words sounded like a command.

"I'm gone."

"Please, Frank." Terri reached for him.

He held her hand briefly. "Goodbye, Terri. I'm glad I met you."

As he turned to go, Ted and several other male Friends blocked his path. He tightened up to make a run for the car. To his relief, Alpha interceded.

"Let him go. He's not one of us. He doesn't belong here. He doesn't deserve to be one of us."

Frank pushed through. They crowded around as he got in the car. He glared at them through the closed window and started the engine. Pulling away, he tried to see Terri among the crowd but couldn't. Some of them bumped against the car and threw gravel at it. He flipped them off.

"Go to hell, Friends."

He was glad to be in the safety of his car. Things had turned sour quickly. Jaw set, he drove away without a backward glance. When he finally reached the highway, he turned back south toward the Imperial Valley and pushed the Toyota as hard as he dared. It felt great to be back on the road.

"All right." He turned the radio to a country station and cranked up the volume, "I'm outta here."

5

TUCSON HAD CHANGED SINCE FRANK had last seen it, but only superficially. There were a couple of new high rises downtown, some new, fast, wide roads stretching across the city, and innumerable small, no doubt short-lived businesses lining the streets, but overall it was the same sprawling little big town it had been for the last decade or two.

After the 'Friends,' he intended to visit another of his old home towns and see Scott Welch, one of his best friends from long past University of Arizona days. He drove straight through from Indio with only a quick stop in Yuma before the long, barren, but to him, beautiful haul to Tucson. He took the Speedway exit and headed east through town. It was good to take a breather from the road, even though he was beginning to get into a highway rhythm.

Scott lived in one of the older neighborhoods on the east side of town in a one floor, brick, ranch-style home built in the early 60s when Tucson was in fact a little one-horse town. That Scott was buying the house was a conspicuous sign of how far he'd come since his impoverished student teaching days at the U of A.

He was just finishing dinner opened the door with a piece of pizza in his hand. "Frankie, my man, how the hell are you?"

"Whatya say, bud?"

"How long's it been? Two, three years?"

"Four, I think. Yeah, four."

"God, I can't believe it."

"Well, it's been a while."

"It's so good to see you. Come on in."

"I was hopin' you'd ask."

"Say, can I talk you into some pepperoni pizza? I got plenty left."

"No, no. I'm not hungry."

"Oh, hell, I damn near forgot. Sorry. You're still eating rabbit food, I bet."

"Right. Don't worry about it. I try not to inflict my eating habits on others."

"What was that we used to say? All you ate was grass and...."

"Grass and twigs. All I eat is grass and twigs."

"That's it. Same old Frank."

"Same old."

"Okay." Scott pushed away the last few pieces of pizza on the kitchen counter. "You've been here long enough. What'll it be? Beer, wine, weed?"

"All of the above."

"Right on."

———

"I JUST DON'T LIKE THE American left." Frank argued over his fifth beer. "It's too cliquish, too elitist, too full of rich kids pretending to be revolutionaries, too full of people vying for most radical of the year. All the games wore me out. They were boring. *It* was boring."

"Human politics, that's all. You take that side of it too seriously and let your own ego get in the way. Just ignore the bull and keep working. That's the way it works. That's the way it'll succeed someday. You gotta stay in it for the long haul, buddy, put the crap out of your mind, ignore the trivial, stay for the duration. You dig, my man?"

"Yeah, I dig."

"Well, then, come in from the cold. Get back into it. We need all the people we can get."

"You mean be a pacifist. Be on the liberation theology God squad?"

"You once believed in pacifism."

"Once. I'm too much of a coward to keep believing in it. You have to have more guts than I do to let them pound your ass all the time."

"There are alternatives to pacifism."

"You mean direct action."

"That's one."

"The truth is I'm too afraid of prison and dying to do something really radical. And I sure ain't into no UPG."

"UPG? What the heck is that?"

"Useless Personal Gesture. The one where a single person does something crazy and gets put away or blown away for it. Unless there's a mass movement, it's all a bunch of UPGs. Especially now, I mean, hell, there ain't even a Soviet Union anymore or any commies hardly left. Why should I be out banging the gong for the left when the Goddamned left has given up on itself. I mean if the Bolsheviks have dumped it, what in the hell am I hanging on for?"

"You're just rationalizing non-commitment, dude. You're selling yourself and your beliefs short. And you're taking the short term historical approach. Listen, Marxist-Leninist crap may be way down, but it ain't out."

"Could have fooled me."

"Hang around. It ain't over till it's over."

"Listen, I still believe in the left. I just feel estranged from it, that's all. I support the causes, the ideals. It's the people I don't want to be around."

"Maybe it's not them. Maybe it's you."

"No deal. Fifty-fifty at best. Them and me. I don't buy the 'I'm not committed and everyone else is' routine."

"But you really aren't committed, man. How long has it been since you did anything for the movement? Years?"

"What am I supposed to do, join M-19 in Colombia—never mind, they're probably gone, too, now. Maybe I should throw myself onto a live death squad in Central America, or how about spending the rest of the only life I have gettin' hammered by a mass murderer? It's better to be taken out in a firefight than to get thrown in the slammer."

"Excuses. Oldest in the book. You can do better than that."

"Okay, so I'm an abject coward. I said I was. So what? I'm in my mid-forties, man. I don't have that much time left. When I was younger that didn't seem so critical somehow. It's just now all I can think of is trying to enjoy myself a little, maybe. It's not like I've led this really wasteful, degenerate life, you know."

"Yeah, I know. Nobody's saying you haven't done things or had things done to you. I know your past. There's a lot you can be proud of, but you have to stay with it, man, all the way. Otherwise, you're just another *compañero*, another fellow traveler."

"You don't hear that much anymore. They haven't made it against the law to talk about this stuff yet, have they?"

"Come on. Get back in the swing of things. I'll be your mentor. As a matter of fact, you couldn't have come at a better time."

"What does that mean?" Frank tilted his head to get a clean look at Scott's face.

"Now don't prejudge and bail out before I finish my proposal."

"Proposal? What are you talking about?"

"Well, I work with AYUDA—you know, the Christians that help refugees from Central America?"

Frank raised a skeptical eye. "I know."

"Wait a second, hear me out. Me and another guy are making a run for them tomorrow night."

"*What?*"

"Take it easy, take it easy."

"You're inviting me to make an AYUDA run? You want me to risk jail time on a spur of the moment decision? You're crazy."

"Now hold on. Here's the rest of it. We're just decoys."

"Decoys?"

"Yeah, me and a couple of legal Salvadorans. The Border Patrol sees us in a van with a couple of Hispanics, and they'll go right for us."

"Right for us? Wonderful."

"Sure, it'll be too much to resist."

"Depends on who's resisting what."

"C'mon, you'll like it. It'll be like old times, bring you back to life inside. Feel the old commitment, the old energy. Get it, man?"

"Oh, I'll get it, all right. I been there before, remember?"

"We need you. You have to be on our side. And stay on it. What do you say?"

Frank stared at his feet. "Damn."

6

MANAGUA, NICARAGUA – 1985

TRIP LOG: FRANK MASON

Day 1: Aeromexico on milk run—Tucson to Hermosillo, Ciudad Obregon, Culiacan, Guadalajara, Mexico City—overnight at the Quaker's Casa de Los Amigos

Day 2: TACA Airlines to San Salvador and Managua. Greeted by giant picture of Sandino at the airport looking like Tom Mix.

Day 3: Staying with pro-Sandinista Savala family in Barrio Maximo Jerez. Dirt floors, cots in tiny, partitioned sleeping areas. Indoor water from a single, narrow pipe for showers—huge water bugs and incongruous U. S. disco music on the radio.

Day 4: Tour of Managua. Poorest country since Korea in service.

Day 5: Language classes by day; the bar El Radial by night, beer served in containers you have to bring yourself.

Day 6: Protest at U. S. Embassy, CIA types just beyond fence to Embassy compound; Duo Guardabarranco in the evening.

Day 7: Mercado Oriental—black market countering official goods/prices of Sandinista run Mercado Roberto Huembes.

Day 8: Tour to El Coral, at edge of Contra activity in the countryside. Sandinista guards on bus, real cowboys, country music.

Day 9: Bus to Granada, Lake Nicaragua. Drunk Miskito Indian drafted into Sandinista army. At home—a hot tortilla with cream sauce, perfect antidote to the Revenge.

Day 13: School—propaganda session: how to answer questions upon return to States

Day 14: Good Friday in Leon. Procession in the streets, Roman re-enactors with whips beating first Christians, Calvary replayed in an empty field, Christ and two thieves, energetically portrayed. The beach at Poneloya, Sandinista soldiers on R & R from the front.

Day 15: The beach at Pochomil—beer, cheese snacks, very cold water.

Day 16: Somoza's Revenge maxes out; visited with anti-Sandinista store owner; reading Marge Piercy's *Dance the Eagle to Sleep*

Day 17: Perfect supper of rice, fried bananas, cheese and coarse bread.

Day 19: Preparing to leave—Aeromexico mixup with ticket; visit to the newspaper *El Nuevo Diario*; friends, drinks and snacks at the ironically named *Yerba Buena* café.

Day 20: To *La Prensa* newspaper, then on to Mercado Roberto Huembes for souvenirs.

Day 21: Collecting huge bag of letters and packages to mail back in U. S.; Aeronica flight to Mexico City confirmed; presents and leftovers for Savala family; *"El Auto Fantastico"* ("*Knight Rider*") on Sandinista-approved TV.

Day 22: Aeronica from Managua to Mexico City; bland cheese sandwich and glass of milk; Mexicana Airlines, Mexico City to Los Angeles; met by cousins, ate veggie burger at Larry Parker's in Beverly Hills—serious culture shock.

Day 23: America West, Burbank to Phoenix to Tucson, bumpy air during final landing approach. Central American trip over. Political, personal and work life in Tucson remains uncertain, unsettled, unsure.

7

THE BORDER PATROL LET THE van get out of Nogales and onto I-19 before they made their move. In the fading light, Frank saw them coming, making out the familiar lime-colored vehicles—a Jeep and a car—in the rider's side mirror.

"Here they come." He tried for a matter of fact tone but failed.

"I got 'em." Scott checked the rear view mirror. Alfredo and Omar, two decoy, legal Salvadorans, sat in back. "From here on act as natural as possible. We're just average citizens who've been to Nogales, Sonora, and now we're going back to Tucson. *Me Entienden?* Understand?" The men nodded.

"*Muy bien.* Everybody stay cool."

"They got their lights on now, this is it."

"Okay." Scott slowed the van. "I'm gonna pull over. Stay calm."

The Border Patrol stopped behind them, Jeep in back, car in front. There were four agents, one stayed in the Jeep, the other three surrounded the van, hands near their holstered weapons.

"Evening, sir." A tall, middle-aged agent addressed Scott. "Could we see some identification, please?"

The second agent, a stout young man, asked the same of Frank. Frank fumbled in his billfold for his driver's license.

The third agent, a Hispanic, was somewhere behind the van.

"Is there some problem, officer?" The second officer saw the Salvadorans. He signaled to the older agent.

"Would you please step out of the van slowly and ask those two gentlemen in the back to get out also."

"Sure." Scott immediately complied. "But what have we done?"

"Just step down, please, and show us your hands. We need to see your hands. Two men are coming out the back, Gilbert." The older agent called back to his partner covering the van from behind.

"They're mine." Alfredo and Omar climbed out.

In the glaring headlights of the car, the seven men stood in back of the van, the agents carefully scrutinizing all IDs with long, heavy flashlights. Cars whooshed by on the interstate, and a dog barked in the distance. For a moment the whole scene transformed into a still life with flashing lights.

"They're all legal." The young, stocky agent told the older one. "Everything squares up." The older agent handed Scott his ID.

"I'm not altogether sure. . . ."

"Hey, hey, Cliff." The fourth agent interrupted, leaning out the driver's side of the Jeep. "Come here."

The older agent walked back to the Jeep, conferred for a moment with the driver, then rejoined the group behind the van.

"Seems we missed an actual illegal alien run by just a few minutes, son." He stood close to Scott. "You wouldn't know anything about that, would you?"

"Oh, no, sir, we were just down in Nogales shopping."

"Maybe we should check for drugs." The Hispanic agent shone his light in Frank's face.

"No, these boys are too smart for that, aren't you?"

"Uh, yes, sir."

"It was a decoy." The young agent was not pleased. "We oughta run these guys in, anyway."

"Nah, waste of time. It'd get tossed out of court."

"You people are lucky. I'd like to haul you in."

"Are we free to go?"

"Cliff?"

"Give them their IDs."

"Thank you, officer." Scott and Frank took back their driver's licenses.

Alfredo and Omar hopped back in the van. The agents shut the door. Frank hurried to the rider's side and Scott climbed into the driver's seat. The older agent waited until everyone was in, then he leaned in Scott's window.

"You boys got away with this one." His voice was low but the message strong and clear. "Next time you might not be so lucky. I don't expect to see you again."

"No, sir. Not again. Thank you."

Frank squirmed in his seat.

"That's fine."

The older agent walked to the Border Patrol car and got in. The two vehicles immediately pulled out and crossed over the median to the southbound lanes of the interstate. They turned off their flashing lights and headed back toward Nogales.

"Hot damn." Scott turned to do sitting high fives with Alfredo and Omar. "We did it."

Frank slumped against the door. "Jesus Christ, I can't believe it's over. Scott, you are one crazy mother."

8

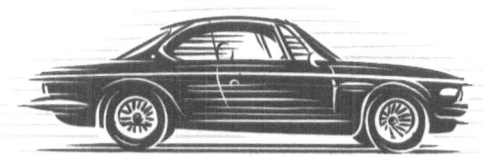

SURE YOU WON'T STAY, BUDDY?" Scott watched Frank toss his day bag into the Toyota. "The movement could sure use you. We need all the hands we can get."

Frank leaned against the car. "Not just now. I'm not ready yet."

"Hey, it was fun, though, wasn't it? We pulled one off—the refugees made it."

"It was a little too much fun for me. I'm an old man, remember."

"Baloney. You're cool."

"You're too optimistic, too upbeat."

"And you're acting dead before your time. Come on, stay here a while longer. We'll bring you back to life. This is what life is, man. The struggle."

"There are other kinds of struggles, Scott."

"I hear you But don't let that make you forget the real one, the main one."

"You really believe in this rising from the ashes bull, don't you?"

"Stronger and better. Democratic, socialist. That's the new phoenix, bud, mark my words."

"You are a piece of work, my friend."

"Don't stay away so long. I'll introduce you to some movement girls."

"I'll be by again, *amigo.*"

Scott stepped up and the men hugged. "Okay, pal, until later. *Nos vemos.*"

"*Nos vemos.*" Frank slid into the driver's seat and started the engine. Scott pointed at the pack of Marlboros on the dash.

"You start smoking again, you crazy dude?"

"No." He tossed them onto the front seat beside him. "Don't know why I have them."

"Let me know what happens to you."

Frank eased away from the curb. He waved. "Read about it in the papers."

Scott gave him a thumbs up sign.

Driving slowly down to the end of the block, Frank saw Scott in the rear view mirror. At the corner, he made a left and then his friend was out of sight. He settled back into the seat. At the next big intersection, he took another left and followed Kolb Road past the back entrance to computer giant GCSI's big Tucson plant and on out to the interstate. Making another left onto the ramp, he was soon cruising along with the rest of the traffic on eastbound I-10.

"Okay." He announced, as if he were piloting a private jet instead of his dumpy little Toyota. "Next stop, Boulder, Colorado."

9

A FTER THE BAKING HEAT OF the barren Arizona-New Mexico desert, Colorado was refreshingly cool and pine green. He had gone the way he always did. From Tucson to Deming on I-10, then the quick fifty mile jog on Highway 26 to Hatch, across the Rio Grande, and onto I-25 North for the straight haul to Denver.

Maneuvering the Toyota through the continual freeway construction in the Mile-High City, he took the 36 exit to Boulder. Near his destination to the west were the Flatirons—large, grayish slabs of rock on the face of the foothills surrounding the picturesque mountain town. At the first main intersection, he took a right, found a grocery store with pay phones and gave Glenn Harrison a call.

"You're here." His tone seemed less than enthusiastic over Frank's arrival.

"Maybe I caught you at a bad time?"

They went back several years together, having worked first at Tucson's GCSI plant. Glenn had been a new hire, Frank his unofficial mentor. A decent work and social friendship had developed between them and then Glenn had found and married another GCSIer, Trudy Sanders.

Trudy did not like Frank, and the feeling was mutual. She and his ex-wife Laura hadn't hit it off well, either, and after a couple of miserable attempts at social interaction, the men were left with mostly a work-only friendship. They had a beer and watched a ballgame together occasionally, but that was about all.

After two or three years, the couple had transferred to Boulder, and it became a WATS line friendship from there. Still, Glenn had been a decent enough friend, and Frank was willing to run the Trudy gauntlet at least to say hello and maybe have dinner with them. He would prefer just seeing his friend, but he doubted Trudy would go for that, especially now that he was single again and running around to prove it. Single men were frequently considered dangerous by wives, especially clinging wives, and his recent past had done little to recommend him to any stability-seeking wife. Trudy was nothing if not a seeker after stability and security.

"No, no. It's just that we're getting toward the end of a cycle, and the product's on the verge of shipping, so as usual we're busy. But it's normal. You know the routine."

"Yeah, I sure do."

"So, man, what's it like being footloose and fancy free? No wife, no job, no responsibility?"

"No income."

"Right. So where are you?"

"I'm at a King Super in Boulder. Arapahoe and something. 30th, maybe. Across from the mall."

"Well, listen, bud, you want to get together?"

"Uh, that was sort of the idea."

"Yeah, okay. I can't get off before five or so, and neither can Trudy, but we want to see you."

"Right."

"We could meet at the Pearl Street Mall, by the Boulder Book Store, say about six-ish. Could you find something to do till then, kill a little time?"

"Not a problem. There's lots of stuff to do. I can catch up a little on the town. Hang out some, whatever."

"Cool. I'll call Trudy. She'll be real excited you're in town."

"Uh-huh." Frank made a face at the phone's receiver.

"About six, then?"

"Six it will be."

"*Later, pal.*"

"Later, Glenn."

———

"WELL, WHAT DO YOU THINK of 'The Peoples' Republic' today?"

Frank set his veggie burger down. Outside, beyond the stained glass window of the Golden Earth Health Food Restaurant, a University of Colorado coed went roller-blading by.

"Not much of a people's republic anymore, I wouldn't think, not if you compare it to the old days or to Santa Cruz."

"Thank heavens." Trudy made a face.

"They sure got rid of most of the freaks."

"I don't think that's what they were trying to do."

"No?"

"That wasn't it, Frank. The city just voted to control growth, that's all. The times changed. That's where the longhairs went."

"That all happened a long time ago." Trudy reminded Frank.

"That's true, but I remember coming out here when they shut down the crash pads and the churches, left the people on the street."

"I, for one, was glad they did. It was really a drag with all those hippies on the streets all the time, panhandling and getting stoned."

Glenn gave her a look she ignored or didn't understand.

"I forgot you lived up here back then, Trudy. I've always thought of you as a Tucson native."

"She started up here with GCSI," Glenn said. "She really knew what was going on back then."

"Yeah, well, I happened to be one of those 'hippies' on the streets back then, as you say, for a while."

Trudy stirred her plain yogurt and orange juice smoothie.

"It's a different world now." Glenn mediated. "All that's ancient history."

"Pretty much so."

"Good riddance."

Frank restrained an impulse to reach over and slap Trudy's smug face.

"Say, honey, we're failing as hosts. Frank's been in town all day, we should give him the grand tour."

"How about Niwot?" Trudy cracked wise. Glenn giggled.

"Niwot?"

"You know, the little town out on the diagonal between here and Longmont. It's real near the plant."

"Oh, yeah, I forgot about that place. Nice one, Trudy."

"How about the plant?"

"GCSI?" Glenn quizzed.

"Why not? It's where we spend most of our lives."

"I think Frank has probably seen enough of GCSI for a lifetime, huh, bud?"

"I'd say."

Trudy shrugged her shoulders and sucked down the rest of her smoothie. Frank felt a twinge of nausea.

Glenn snapped his fingers. "I got it, let's go for a walk through the mall. It's Friday night. There'll be lots of stuff going on. What do you say, guys? It'll be fun."

Trudy rolled her eyes.

Frank laughed. "Sure, why not?"

———

THE PEARL STREET MALL WAS crowded with kids, couples and singles, meandering past the shops, restaurants, and performers in a dense display of Boulder's leading product—well-heeled students and white collar workers. Frank and the Harrisons strolled along, taking in the sights and sounds of conspicuous enjoyment, upper middle class style. A juggler performed for a while, then a rope walker, and a couple of singers doing worn out John Denver Colorado songs.

All along the mall, Frank searched the buildings for signs of life as it had been when he was here long ago, nearly twenty years before. It could have been a millennium for all he could recognize. All the old head shops and leather stores down Broadway toward the university were gone, and the grimy old Colorado Hotel, once his dingy low-down home, had passed into the same black hole the freaks had disappeared through. God, how could a town be so different?

"Hey, man." Glenn broke into Frank's thoughts. "See that place over there?"

"Huh?"

"I said see that place over there?"

"Where?"

"The one by the clothing store."

"Yeah, what about it?"

"It's a sushi bar. Me and you tomorrow, boys' night out. Can you dig?"

"Sushi bar? Fish?"

"Tomorrow?" Trudy screwed up her face. She might have been imagining having to put Frank up for at least one and maybe two nights. He could swear he saw a shudder pass over her body.

"They got veggie stuff, too, man." Glenn seemed blissfully unaware of his wife's reaction. "No problem. We'll have a blast."

"Aren't we having fun now?" Trudy wanted to know.

"You bet and lots of it. Right, pal?" Glenn punched Frank on the arm.

"Maxed out fun." He feigned a counterpunch and winked at Trudy. "Over the top."

She scrunched up her shoulders and gave them a look that would paralyze a scorpion. Frank leaned his head back and let out a belly laugh.

1 0

BOULDER, COLORADO—1972

R ALPH LEE, OWNER AND MANAGER of Lee's Garbage Collection, checked Frank out from his long hair, dirty shirt and blue jeans to his worn out service brogans.

"Son, I don't give two hoots to a ruptured owl how a man appears. I just want somebody who's willing to work."

"I need a job, Mr. Lee. I gotta make a living."

"Call me Ralph. We ain't formal here. We're working men."

"Thanks, Ralph. I'm willing to work."

"I believe you, but there's a couple of other things we oughta get straight. Number one, when you work on the garbage route, you gotta tie your hair back. If it gets caught in the compacter, it'll rip your head off."

"I'll definitely tie it back, no sweat. I think I'll keep my head for a while."

"I expect you would. Pay's two-fifty an hour. Not great, but better'n a lot."

To a man with four dollars in his pocket and no food in his roach-infested room, two-fifty an hour sounded okay.

"Also, I don't know how long it'll last. We got some contracts coming up, and if we get 'em, the job'll be there. If not, I can't promise you anything permanent."

"Hey, it's okay by me. When do I start?"

"Monday. You'll be with Snuffy Headon."

"Snuffy Headon?"

"My best man. He knows more about garbage than any man in Boulder. He'll train you."

"Okay, see you Monday."

"Seven a.m."

"On the money."

"Atta, boy."

Monday morning it snowed eighteen inches. For an eternity of four and a half hours, Frank stumbled, staggered, and reeled through back yards and driveways lugging impossibly heavy trash cans out to the street to dump in the back of the truck. His brogans were soaking wet within a half hour, and by nine his jeans were frozen from the cuffs to just below the knees.

Through it all, Snuffy kept up a cheerful banter, howling at Frank's mistakes. Just before lunch, he was overjoyed when Frank, his legs buckling beneath him, tossed the contents of an overstuffed can onto his own head and shoulders. Snuffy reared his fat little head back on his fat little shoulders and cut loose a mighty, snaggle-toothed laugh.

"You'll get the hang of it, boy." He declared at lunch. "It just takes time. Took me some time to get really used to it."

He was chowing down on two big hamburgers and a large order of fries. Frank splurged on a small order of fries and small coke to go with his plain bread, two slices of bologna sandwich. While Snuffy ate, he thought about his first paycheck, still in the distant future, and the steaming pepperoni pizza it would buy.

"It gets better from here. This here snow'll probably be gone tomorrow. That's the way it is around here. Comes hard, goes fast."

"God." Frank knocked melting ice off his jeans. "I hope so."

In the afternoon things did get better. The snow began to melt, the houses were farther apart, the cans didn't seem so heavy, and they did a subdivision where the garbage had to be put out by the road in trash bags. That was heaven. Frank thought it should be made a federal law. With a little more free time, Snuffy became voluble, talking about his past and giving a guided tour of Boulder's garbage and the people who discarded it.

"Up here." He pointed to a white Craftsman house in a middle class neighborhood near the university. "This guy'll have a case of empties in his trash can. Day in and day out."

Frank took the lid off and counted. There were twenty-one empty beer cans.

"Close enough for government work."

"Told you."

"Yep."

Over the next couple of weeks, they struck up a comfortable workingman's relationship. Snuffy taught Frank how to use his legs to take the weight off the back when carrying heavy cans out of Boulder's uphill backyards. He gossiped about the lady who perfumed her garbage, the man who tried to hide his male pinup magazines at the bottom of his trash can, the couple who liked to parade back and forth naked in front of their uncurtained bedroom window when the garbagemen came by. Within a week, Frank had seen it all for himself.

For his part, he began to feel a little at home in Boulder and enjoyed his partner's unregenerate nosiness in the thrown away parts of people's lives. To enliven the day, he told Snuffy about being a freak—drugs, sex, and rock and roll, man. Most of it he made up or had heard about, his own life being far too boring to talk about, and the old garbageman greedily absorbed the tales of life among the new lost generation. Frank didn't mind stretching things a bit. It didn't hurt anything. It made Snuffy happy, and it juiced up the pauper's existence he lived. Useful fictions, he remembered a phrase he'd heard in some class somewhere.

And then it occurred to him that things were going entirely too well. He instinctively felt uncomfortable, distrustful. Something was bound to happen. On the Wednesday morning of his third week, it did. Ralph called him into the office and closed the door. One look at the boss and it was time to start figuring if he had enough money to get back to his girlfriend in Missouri. The contracts fell through. Just as he was afraid of. He was sorry. Frank was sorry, too.

Ralph paid him for an extra couple of days, told him to come back again later in the spring, that he was a decent man, that he would hire him again. Frank was sure he was was sincere. He appreciated it. He took the check. Snuffy had already gone out on the morning run.

"Damn it. We never even said goodbye."

He walked out the front door, glanced up and down Pearl, then turned left toward the scummy hotel. He shrugged his shoulders and coughed for no reason. Boulder was over. Just like that. Finished.

11

GLENN EMPTIED THE HOT SAKE jar into their cups and ordered another round of the potent rice wine. Frank shoveled down kelp-wrapped chunks of white rice and celery and eyed a pretty brunette sitting at a nearby table.

He motioned for Glenn to move. "Scoot a little. I can't see."

"See what?"

"Her."

The girl made eye contact but looked away noncommittally. Glenn twisted his neck to see.

"Jesus Christ. Why don't you just turn around and stare at her."

"Oh, God. She is beautiful."

"Wouldn't you like to get something like that, just once in your life?"

The waiter brought the next jar of sake. Glenn filled his cup until it spilled down the sides.

"Dude, don't waste this. It's some good stuff."

"Bet you drank a lot of this over in the Philippines or wherever it was you were."

"Japan and Korea." Frank adopted the semi-tough veteran's attitude he liked to use when he got a little drunk in a safe place.

"I bet those were the days, huh?"

"They were okay." Frank filtered out the myriad bad memories that always popped up when he thought about his service days for long. "These are better."

"You really think so?"

"No." They both laughed. The brunette and her boyfriend looked over. Frank winked at the girl. They both faced the other way.

"Piss off." He muttered.

"Don't get mad. Let's go somewhere else and get rowdy."

"I'm not mad."

"Sure you are. You're mad a lot these days. You say so yourself when we talk on the phone. Trudy said—"

"Humph. Did Trudy say whatever it was she said before or after she chased us the hell out on our boy's night out?"

"That's not fair. We were saying that you're bound to be really angry at everything right now."

"Thanks for sharing that. Glad you and your loving spouse have me analyzed so well."

"We're concerned about you. We're your friends."

"Sorry. Sometimes I am mad. Really mad. I'm not always happy with my little lot in life."

"Yeah, but you did manage to finally quit GCSI. You hit the road and are buzzing all around on your own. You're free now. A free agent. You should be getting happy again. Me, I'm stuck at GCSI forever. Trudy and I are bored to death with each other, and I got nothing but mortgages and loans to forever. Work. Work. I work all the time. You know."

The brunette and her boyfriend got up to leave.

"I know." Frank checked out the girl as she passed by. She returned a peripheral glance. The boy stared straight ahead.

"Nah, come on. You know."

"Yeah, I'm sorry. I do know."

And he did know. He knew about jobs and how they could become the real drug of your choice. It started as just work and then you aged and started losing things. Your youth, your commitment, your integrity, your wife. Then soon, work was all you had. All there was. It was your identity. It was who you were.

It was all you were. No wonder he was angry much of the time. No wonder he'd dropped out and split from San Diego.

"What do you mean you and Trudy are bored to death with each other?"

"You weren't listening, were you? You didn't hear me."

"Of course I heard you. I said I know, didn't I? I heard the part about you and Trudy, didn't I?"

"No, no, I asked if you wanted to go. You were ogling that girl. It's getting late, and Trudy's expecting us back at the house."

He set his cup of sake down abruptly. Its effect on him had suddenly weakened. He looked over clear-eyed at Glenn. Another short trip to Boulder was apparently coming to an end. It just wasn't meant to be his town.

"I made my choices." He pushed the cup away. "And I should be happy with them. Right?"

"I was under the impression it was what you wanted, Frank. To be free."

"Sometimes you have to give up a lot to be free. It's a high price to pay."

"I believe you." Glenn waved the waiter over. "Could we have the bill, please?"

The waiter bowed and went for the ticket.

Frank leaned back and folded his arms across his chest. He'd always liked Glenn, but he realized now that their friendship could never expand beyond the boundaries set by GCSI, by Trudy, by the void of experience between them. He felt a surge of sadness. He knew he wasn't going to stay past the morning. He'd have to stay the night so as not to hurt their feelings, but he was already gone in his mind. Sometimes he hated whatever it was about himself that kept basically decent people like Glenn and Trudy forever at arm's length.

Like most everyone else, he had a soft inside under the shell grownups always constructed around themselves. What he hated sometimes was that underneath the human soft spot was another layer of self, another place, a secret place, a place cold and aloof. A place of impenetrable ego, a place no one—no one—could touch.

He felt that place mostly as a semi-conscious sensation.

But at times he saw or felt it clearly—and in that place was no fear, no pain, no joy, no pleasure, no feeling at all. No feeling for friends, for loved ones, for family, maybe not even for himself.

He stood up just as the waiter returned with their bill. They tossed some money on the little plate the man held until he seemed satisfied and retired again.

Glenn stood. "Ready?"

"Ready to go."

Glenn patted his friend on the shoulder as they headed out of the restaurant. Frank didn't notice, he was already a long way down the interstate in his mind.

12

JAKE WILLIAMS MOVED HIS SOLID midwestern frame deftly between stalks of corn mingled with occasional marijuana plants.

Behind him, Frank wiped his sweating brow and tried to avoid breaking any of the weed—or corn. The Missouri sun beating down on them was intense enough on its own, but in the humid, thick field, it was virtually tropical.

"Damn, it's hot in here." He stumbled between rows.

"Nice plants, ain't they, Frankie?"

"Jeez. I feel like I'm in an outdoor steam bath down here. The plants do okay in this, dude?"

"Missouri weed's as good as anybody else's. Must be okay."

"Yeah, but it's not 'Missouri' Missouri weed, right? I mean it's Acapulco Gold or Panama Red or whatever everybody used to call it, you know?"

"It's a Thai-Cambodian mix if you're wanting to get technical." Jake combed back a stray blond lock of thinning hair with his right hand. "It's very strong."

They walked further through the plants, rubbed the leaves on several robust marijuana stalks.

"You know, Jake, I really like it out here, and you know I love getting out in the country, but I don't mind telling you it makes me nervous as hell being around all these weed plants."

"As it should, man. You got the makings of a dope farmer."

"I'm serious, dude."

"I hear you. But you gotta have a little fear, or you'll screw up and get busted."

"I thought they had special ways of detecting this stuff from the air now."

"They do."

"Well, how in the hell do you keep from getting busted?"

"You don't plant a solid field of it. You don't plant too much in any one area. You rotate the crops. Just like any other kind of farmer."

"And there's still a market for all this? I thought most of it died out with all us dinosaur pot heads."

"Come on, you know better'n that. Despite the 'Just Say No' crap, weed's really been institutionalized. Ever have any trouble getting any?"

"Well, lately, yeah."

"C'mon, you can't get it in California?"

"Well, if I try."

"There you are."

"I know you're right, but I forget sometimes. Everybody seems so damned straight these days it's hard to imagine them tokin' up on a jay. Know what I mean?"

"But that's exactly who's firin' up now." Jake paused in the field to smell a stray flower accidentally growing among the corn and marijuana. "Isn't it great out here?" He inhaled deeply of the flower's fresh fragrance.

Frank looked around at the sun-flooded fields beyond the crops to a small stand of sycamore trees, then above to the deep blue Missouri sky. He felt the heat, the humidity. He smelled the corn, the weed, even the soil. It was home in a way that he could sense strongly, but only in a flash in moments like these. It was a past he thought he understood, but could not recapture for his own.

"I love it here. I miss it sometimes. A lot."

"It's where we came from, Frankie." Jake stretched his arms out. "It's where we belong. It's what we were meant to be. Not factory workers, not slaves to computers, none of that. We were meant to be out here. This is what's real. This is the whole point."

He bent over and put a calloused hand into the dirt, pulling up a crumbling chunk of earth. He ground it to dust with his fingers and let what vague breeze there was return it to the soil from which it came. For a few moments he stood still and breathed in the world around him. It smelled clean, fresh. It was hot and humid but this was indeed what man was meant to do—farm. It didn't matter if it was corn or wheat or weed. Yeah, Jake was right, this was it.

"Hell." Jake's voice wrenched Frank from the contemplation of a golden agrarian age that likely never existed. A car was pulling into the front yard behind his Toyota.

"Who is it?" Frank failed to hide the fear in his voice. "Cops?"

"Oh, no, they'd never come this time of day."

"Right, they'd only be comin' if it was about four-thirty in the morning, and they'd be en masse and sneakin' up."

"Exactly."

"A friend?"

"Not one you'd want to claim, probably."

"Oh, the man."

"The man. 'The' man. Let's head back. He likes punctuality."

"No doubt. Should I split?"

"No, it'll be okay. Vince is business-like. He won't like seeing you—he doesn't like seeing anybody he doesn't know—but it's not a problem."

"If you say so."

Two men got out of the car, a light blue Cordoba.

"Who's who?"

"Vince is the thinner guy in the pullover shirt. The guy with the jacket is Mal, his, uh, driver."

"Terrific." Frank swallowed as the four of them met at the side of Jake's simple pre-fab house.

"Whad'ya say, Vince?" Jake shook Vince's white, clean hand.

Vince smiled thinly. Frank tried to seem as dumb, friendly, and non-threatening as humanly possible. He could feel the driver's gaze sizing him up. He resisted an urge to shift his weight from one foot to the other.

"Oh, Vince, I want you to meet an old, old buddy of mine. Frank Mason. Frank, Vince."

"How ya doin'?" Vince extended a ringed hand.

"Good to meet you." The soft pressure of the handshake was surprising. "I'm not that old, Jake."

Jake chuckled, Frank snickered, and Vince revealed a set of perfect, probably capped teeth. The driver was impassive. Vince didn't introduce him. That was okay with Frank.

"You live around here?" Vince asked Frank.

"Oh, no, no, I'm just traveling through. Just stopped by to see Jake for a little while."

"Very nice."

"Let's go in, gentlemen." Jake opened the front door.

They headed inside, Jake and Frank first, then Vince. Mal, the driver, came in last and stood by the door.

Vince settled on a big, heavy couch. "And how's the product?"

Jake motioned for Frank to take a seat. He sat down gingerly on the edge of a thickly padded Barcalounger. All of the furniture was big, solid—permanent. It was comfortable, but too rooted down.

"How 'bout a beer, Vince?"

"Sure."

"Frank?"

"I'll get 'em." Frank hopped up, glad to be out of the too comfortable chair. He peeked over at Mal. Mal didn't move a muscle.

"He never drinks." Vince explained. "He's my driver."

"Oh, heh, heh, I see."

He hurried out to the kitchen. When he got back with the beers, Jake was explaining to Vince where they stood with this year's 'product.' Mal had been watching out the window and turned back toward the middle of the room as Frank handed out the beer.

"If the weather holds, we should have about one and a half times what we had last year, Vince. I got a buttload more plants out there this time."

"Excellent." Vince's voice was flat, humorless.

Frank sat on the edge of the Barcalounger and tried to check out boss and his driver without appearing to do so. They seemed like classic ex-cons to him and for several minutes he was preoccupied with fantasies about arrests and shootouts. In the middle of a mental fight in which he was wrestling a .357

away from Mal, an unwelcome, extraneous sound drifted into his conscious-
ness. He didn't immediately recognize it, but it grew louder, nearer, more ob-
trusive. Finally, he realized what it was. With a start, he nearly jumped up, then
held himself still. An airplane.

Christ, the cops. It's a cop plane. Busted.

He checked Jake, then Vince, but they acted like they didn't hear anything.
He fought an urge to run to the window, to run out in the yard. The plane sounded nearer yet. Jake and Vince kept talking. Mal was no longer at the front door.
How had the big driver disappeared so quietly, so deftly? He waited a long, tense
minute. The plane noise was diminishing. Mal emerged from the kitchen.

"A couple of miles off." He announced the news casually, resumed his
position by the door.

"Very good, Mal."

Frank relaxed and actually sat back a little in the Barcalounger. Vince
looked over at him, then back at Jake.

"Okay, everything seems cool here. I'll tell my people the news."

"Right on."

How far had that phrase come in fifteen, twenty years? Frank blew a breath
out of the side of his mouth. Vince and Jake stood up. Frank popped up. Mal
put a big hand on the front doorknob. Frank felt joy returning to his life.

Vince didn't let him feel it for long. "So, you're just passing through and
stopped to see your old friend, eh?"

"Yeah, yeah, that's right." Frank mustered up the heaviest Okie accent he
could under the circumstances. Maybe being raised a hillbilly had its advantag-
es after all. He tried to appear as disinterested and unaware as possible. "Yep,
just dropping by. Gotta leave in the morning."

"Good plan. This country isn't for everyone. It's a different kind of thing
around here."

"Couldn't agree with you more."

Vince looked at Mal. The driver opened the door. The interview was over.
He'd been 'advised.' A word to the wise.

"See you next month." Vince strode toward the door.

"Sure you don't want a tour of the fields?"

"I'm sure it will be fine, if you say so."

"Okay." Jake thumbed the stubble on his chin. "Be seein' you, Vince. So long, Mal."

The big driver, following his boss directly out the door, said nothing.

"See you." Frank called after them cheerfully.

He and Jake stood at the door, watched the pair walk to the Cordoba. Mal opened and shut the door for Vince. In a moment, the car turned around in the front yard and headed back down the road. When the long sleek machine disappeared around a bend, Frank let out a relieved whistle.

"Jesus Christ, Jake. This is the kind of assholes you have to deal with?"

Jake winked.

"Christ Almighty. That Mal guy was carrying heat, you know?"

"What?"

Jake laughed and soon Frank joined in. He couldn't help himself. He laughed until he was out of breath, until he thought he was going to be sick.

13

W ANT ANOTHER HIT?"
Frank waved off the half-smoked joint. "I've had enough, man, let me take a break for a minute."

Jake laid the number in an ashtray on the living room coffee table. "It's out, anyway."

Frank leaned his kitchen chair back and propped his feet on the edge of the table. He closed his eyes. Jake got up and put on a record, then went to the kitchen for some beers. The sounds of an old Hendrix album filled the blue-smoke filled room. He brought in the beers.

"Remember these tunes?" He proffered a bottle, moved Frank's backpack out of the way and sat on the end of the couch. Grabbing a remote from the table, he clicked on the big heavy TV in the corner of the room and switched it to some old cartoons with the sound down.

"Those were the days, huh, dude?" He took a long drink of beer and let the combination of weed, beer, 'Hey Joe,' and Daffy Duck mix with the still-warm Missouri air and the lingering memory of the afternoon visit with Vince and Mal. He was extremely stoned. "Excellent stuff."

They were quiet for a few minutes. Frank rested his head back and closed his eyes. When he opened them again, Jake gave him a look that combined his honed predisposition toward satire, parody, irony, and sarcasm in a mixture that made him a tough friend to bullshit.

"What? What?"

"What are you running from, Frank? What's up?"

"I ain't runnin' from anything."

"You do something illegal?"

"You, of all people, are asking me that?"

"Well?"

"No. No way."

"You act like you're trying to get away from something. And you were sure jumpy this afternoon. Somebody after you?"

"Nah. Not unless it's me."

"Didn't you like California anymore?"

"I never really liked California. I mean it's okay. San Diego is all right. I just never cared for the whole place. It's too touristy-like, too vacuous. Well, that's not really fair, but, dig, it's still nothing but a pile of dust bowl Okies living in the Promised Land. Second, third, hell, now fourth generation. They've forgotten the old pain, the fear. They only know a material world because that's all that mattered to the old folks."

"Now they're probably panicked by all the Mexicans, Blacks, and Orientals."

"Right."

"Say, pal, did I see some smokes in your bag here?"

"Yeah. Help yourself."

"You start again?"

"No, I don't know why I have them. They been on the dash of my car since El Centro. I finally put them in the bag."

"Can I have one?"

"Of course, crank one up."

"I still like one when I'm really messed up."

"I'm really messed up."

"You really kicked 'em this time?"

"I hope so. But I wish I was like you. Able to smoke one or two now and again. But I can't. One and I'm on the treadmill."

"Spinning on a wheel."

"The wheel. Remember the wheel?"

"The wheel?"

"The wheel of Samsara."

"Oh, God, the Eastern days."

"The wheel of destiny." Frank slid into the old rap. "You stay on the wheel life after life, reincarnated over and over until you reach nirvana. Then you are released from the wheel. The part I liked, to me the interesting and cerebral thing, is that you can only attain nirvana and get off the wheel by not striving for it. You have to reach your goal not by trying for it, but by becoming or being it. Sort of an organic state, you know. It's all part of the oneness, allness and nothingness stuff. In order to be one with all things, which is really nirvana, you must be nothing yet everything all at the same time—without trying. I love that."

Jake nodded his agreement.

"I dug it so much I thought I was on the last stage of the wheel and would reach nirvana."

"Most excellent, dude."

"No kiddin', man. When a westerner like me deals with something like this, nirvana becomes just like the Southern Baptist's heaven."

"That's where the bhodisattvas come in. They kick it all up another notch."

"Right on." Frank took a drink of beer.

"Man, we were really into it."

"I can't believe how much. It's embarrassing in retrospect. The only residue, I think for me, is being a veggie—and refusing to dump on Herman Hesse along with all the program-me-to-make-a-living pseudo-intellectual me generation that's been running rampant for the last fifteen years or so now. I tell you one thing Hesse wrote, though, Jake old buddy, that still sticks with me. It's from *Siddartha*, where Vasudeva says, 'I can think. I can wait. I can fast.' I use that sometimes like a mantra to calm myself down."

"You really studied the whole thing a lot, I guess."

"Not really. I'm just a dilettante. You know me, learn enough to sound convincing. A shallow knowledge of many things. In some places that'll get you by as a Renaissance man. But for me, it's like education in general or Jonathan Winters, a really dangerous thing if you get exposed to it at too young an age."

"You're too much."

"Eastern stuff is interesting though, isn't it?"

"Yeah." Jake stood and walked to the window. It was getting late in the day. "It's not out there on the road, though, my friend."

"Huh?" Frank burned up the rest of the roach between two paper matches. He inhaled deeply, allowing the smoke to envelope his nose and mouth.

"Whatever it is that has driven you out here."

Frank coughed. "This is most excellent weed, man." He hacked.

"Sounds like it."

Frank sniffled and took a throat-soothing swig of beer. For a split second, he felt like the top of his head was going to blow off.

"You can't find yourself on the road because you're already you. You carry yourself wherever you go. The locale changes. You are who you are."

"I hear you, Jake, but the geographical cure can work. It's worked for me in the past. Maybe it'll work again."

"Well, you know, buddy, you're welcome to stay here if you want. There are worse places to work out demons. Besides, I can always use the help."

"Thanks." Frank downed the rest of his beer. "But I should keep on movin'. I don't think this is quite my thing. Too many real demons. Too many traps. Too scary."

"It's not for everyone."

"No, no it isn't."

"Well, I'm glad you came by anyway."

"Me, too."

"And next?"

"I think I'll drop by and see Duane and Mattie in Columbia."

"Sure, they're great people. More reconnecting, huh?"

"I guess so."

Jake lifted a beer in salute to Frank.

"Hope you find what you're after, my friend."

"*Salud*, brother. Amen."

14

FRANK REACHED DUANE AND MATTIE'S place around three-thirty in the afternoon, a little wired and a little tired. But not too much as it had been an unusually cool day and regular, slow moving cumulus clouds had provided refreshing shade throughout the afternoon.

Parking the Toyota just off the half-moon gravel driveway in front of their house, he stepped down into the recently mowed front lawn and stretched his arms and legs. He turned to head for the front door, but a huge German Shepherd came bounding around the side of the house and made a bee line for him.

He froze, muscles tensing and fists clenched, as the dog loped up to him. He stood stock still and the dog stopped directly in front of him, its face at an uncomfortable level with his crotch.

"Good dog." He tried to sound confident and brave.

The dog shuffled back and forth and wagged its tail. He lowered one hand for the dog to sniff, which it did and then proceeded, as big dogs are wont, to smell his pant legs and privates. He knelt and patted the dog on the head, the dog licked him—slobbered him—right in the face.

"You're a sweet dog, aren't you, you big old thing. What's your name?"

The dog responded by practically knocking him over with an excess of tail wagging. He petted and roughed up the hair on the animal's head.

The dog panted happily.

When he looked up from loving the dog, Mattie was standing on the bottom step of the front porch, wearing sandals, blue jeans, and a gray T-shirt. Her light brown hair was pulled back into a pony tail with one stray lock from her bangs hanging in front of her eyes.

It had been a while since he last saw her, but even at this distance, she was still one of the prettiest women he'd ever known. Seeing her again like this, appearing from nowhere, struck him with such force he wondered if he wasn't and hadn't always been in love with her.

She had her cool, penetrating blue eyes zeroed in on him and the dog. He continued patting the dog, but didn't take his eyes off her. "I see you've met Biff."

"What? Biff? You actually named this big old dog Biff?"

The dog jumped around at the sound of his name, again nearly knocking Frank off balance in canine exuberance.

"I'm surprised he hasn't bit all of you out of spite."

Mattie came across the lawn. "For your information, Mr. Smart Alec, he was named by Sara and Paulie. They thought it was a cute, funny name. I happen to agree. And he's an angel of a dog."

"Poor Biffie." He again roughed up the dog's fur. "You should be Conan or Thor. Hell, I thought he was going to kill me when I first saw him."

"Biff? He wouldn't hurt a flea."

"Yeah, well." Frank stepped around Biff toward her. She opened her arms, and they hugged tightly, familiarly, the affection between them undiminished despite the miles and years apart.

"Same old articulate Frankie." She pulled back from him, but held onto his forearms with her hands.

"You never did cut me much slack, did you?"

"Not a character like you."

"Man, it's great to see you again."

"We've missed you, too. All of us have. A lot."

"Me, too."

She put her right arm through his left and guided him toward the house.

"Duane and the kids still at school?" They passed by the front steps. Biff tagged along, hanging out at his side.

"Uh-huh. They'll be home any minute now."

"I can't wait to see them."

"Shall I show you around until they get here?"

"Absolutely."

Arm in arm they walked around the side of the house into a big, also recently mowed back yard.

"We're happy here."

Mattie's direct way of speaking reminded him that with her you always felt like you were the absolute center of her attention. No wonder her men friends always fell in love with her, and no wonder that of all the women he had known, she was his favorite—maybe Kim excepted. She was honest, pretty, intelligent, moral, and seemingly okay with who she was all the time.

"Seems to me you would probably be happy anywhere, as long as you had the kids and Duane."

"Probably so but this is our special place. We have seven and a half acres, a small pond, a horse, a cow, a hen house, and a pigpen—with chickens that don't lay and pigs that don't get eaten. The kids can't bear to have us butcher them. And then there's my pride and joy." She walked him to a large cultivated area beyond the back yard. "The vegetable garden."

The garden had three rows of healthy corn and innumerable rows of lettuce, squash, radishes, carrots, and anything else they wanted to grow.

"That is one major garden."

"We get so much food from it."

"I imagine, don't you have any—"

She interrupted him, turning to point toward the road behind them. "Here come Duane and the kids."

Frank peered beyond the right side of the house. Sure enough, there they came down the road in the family Honda wagon. They hurried back up to the house to greet them. Duane and the kids waved happily when they saw Mattie and then, except for Paulie, the younger of the children, added another burst at the sight of Frank. He waved back and stood by smiling as Duane parked in front of the house.

15

HALFWAY THROUGH SUPPER, SARA NOTICED that Frank didn't have any baked chicken to go with his mashed potatoes and cooked vegetables.

She turned toward Mattie. "Momma, Uncle Frank didn't get any chicken."

"Tha's 'kay." He garbled, shoveling in a large forkful of potatoes and carrots.

Somewhere in the lost regions of his childhood, he had adopted the eating habits of a starving orphan, and he'd never been able to change them. Paulie watched him eat with reverential awe.

"Uncle Frank doesn't eat meat, honey."

Sara turned back to Frank wide-eyed. "Why don't you eat meat?"

Paulie, not sure what was going on, but sure it was important, followed the conversation with his eyes. He shifted his attention from one speaker to the next as if he were at a tennis match.

"Oh, I just don't, Sara." Frank flooded down the vegetables with a big drink of water. "That's all."

"You can tell her the real reasons, Frank. We talk straight to the kids about most everything."

"You really want to know?"

Sara nodded her head. Paulie directed his attention to Frank.

"A long time ago, I was studying a philosophy that talked about how every-thing—people, animals, the earth, everything—was one thing together. Any one thing was as important as everything else, and everything was part of the same thing."

"You mean an animal, like a rabbit or a pig, is as important as a person?"

"Like a pig?" Paulie chimed in.

"Yes, something like that."

"Wow." Sara proclaimed. "How about chickens?"

"Same thing. The idea is that all things living have the right to live, and if we don't need to eat them to live, then there's no reason to."

"What about fruit and stuff? They're living, too, aren't they?"

"Yes, honey." Duane interceded. "But they aren't alive in the same sense as people and animals are. At least they don't seem to be."

"Oh." Sara didn't seem too sure of the distinction being made. She lifted her piece of baked chicken off the plate and set it on a napkin. "Well, I agree with Uncle Frank. I don't want to eat meat anymore either."

Paulie didn't follow Sara's lead, but he stared at his chicken leg like it had just sprouted feathers and was getting ready to fly off his plate.

"Hold on, hon," Frank told Sara, "I was just telling you why I don't eat meat. I don't want you to make an important decision like that without con-sidering it some more. You're real smart kids, but you should wait until you're older and then decide on something like this. Think about it, read about it, and then make your choice. And don't do it just because I do."

Frank checked with Duane, then Mattie. Sara put her chicken back on the plate but only nibbled at it. Paulie had already gone back to gnawing.

"We only eat fish and chicken at home. Mattie told Frank. "We never serve beef. They've never had a hamburger."

"Huh-uh, Mommie." Paulie corrected. "I ate a Big Mac once."

"Oh, my." Frank feigned mock horror. "What a wild boy you are."

Paulie giggled, causing some peas to fall out of his mouth.

"Now me." Frank reached for the little boy's stomach. "I never eat meat except for big, fat, little boys—like you!"

Paulie squealed with delight and nearly knocked his milk over. Duane caught it, but some spilled on the table cloth.

"Settle down." Mattie admonished her youngest. "You're going to make a mess."

"I'm sorry. I tend to get too rowdy with kids sometimes. Sorry, Paulie pal, I got you in trouble."

"It's okay, Duane tousled his son's hair. "They're extra excited because you're here tonight."

"Me, too. It's wonderful to see you all."

"Will you read us a story for bedtime, Uncle Frank?" Sara asked, her child's face bright and happy.

"Me, too." Paulie begged. "Me, too?"

"If it's okay with your mom and dad, you bet. I'd love to."

The kids turned simultaneously to Mattie. "Mom?"

"If Uncle Frank doesn't mind, I don't mind."

"All right by me."

"Hot dog." Sara cheered.

"Meat." Frank teased.

"Hot. . . broccoli." She laughed. Everyone joined her, even Paulie, and he didn't have the slightest idea why.

———

AFTER FRANK READ STORIES TO the kids and they had been tucked safely in bed, the adults went to the family room to visit and watch TV. Frank and Mattie settled on either end of a heavy, comfortable couch in the middle of the room. Duane went to the kitchen for a round of beers. While CNN reported on the former Yugoslavia in the background, Frank and Mattie chatted.

"You got great kids there. You've done a fine job with them."

"Thanks, that's sweet of you to say."

"No, I really mean it."

"Well, they're especially good with you, Frank. They really love you."

"I love them, too. Sara's so smart, and Paulie's a real cute guy. I got a real bang out of him at supper."

"You'd make a wonderful father."

"I've heard that all my life and I appreciate it, but it's absolutely not true. I'm a fun friend, but I'd make a lousy dad."

"Well, whatever. I know we all wish you could live closer to us so we could visit more often."

"Me, too. Maybe I will."

"Except me." Duane returned with the beers. "You'd eat us out of house and vegetable garden and ruin our poor kids' minds with your retrograde commie attitude. And besides you'd be spoonin' my wife, living on my couch, and surfing TV. What's on, anyway?"

"Some report about Boznia-Herzogo-whatever." Frank took the beer Duane offered.

Duane gave Mattie a beer, too, and plopped down on the couch between her and Frank. They watched until the story shifted to a report about fashion models getting cosmetic plastic surgery. Duane lowered the volume on the TV.

"So what do you make of the new world order, anyway, Franko?"

"Don't get me started."

"You don't like the way things are going?" Mattie sipped her beer. "I figured you'd like all the freedom movements popping up everywhere."

"Well, I'm hardly against freedom, but, hell, this crap has just degenerated into nationalism and regionalism—even tribalism. And free to do what? Become a market for useless U.S. and Japanese electronic products? For Pepsis, Big Macs, and Levis? Freedom for whom and for what? All I see is exploding crime rates, civil wars, and people who no longer have an economic backdrop to rely on. What I see is a continent, or a chunk of it, coming apart at the seams."

"Communism failed, that's all." Duane stated. "Now everybody's scrambling to put something in its place. Nationalism seems to be the first thing they've come up with."

"I disagree." Frank waved his beer energetically. "Communism didn't fail. The approach to it and the implementation itself failed, not the philosophy or theory. Hell, all their complaints against capitalism are still completely valid, but their leaders blew their side of it."

"What do you mean?" Mattie asked.

"I mean the failure is with the leadership and the CP cadre—you even saw it here in the U.S. They treated communism like a religion instead of the theory, the model, or the outline that it was. You know, it was all dogma. Adherence to the party line and all that bull. It's a Goddamn guideline, not a law. It should be a dialectic, flexible. And on top of everything else, they mismanaged the living hell out of it. That's why they all fell. Not because of communism itself."

"Spoken like a true Marxist-Leninist in retreat." Duane joked.

"Hardly." Frank took a big drink of beer.

"You ready for another one, Mr. Trotsky?" Frank guzzled the rest of his beer and handed the bottle to Duane. "Mattie?"

"No, I'm fine." Duane hustled off to get more beers.

"Don't you think a little of the free market would improve things over there, though, Frank?"

"To a degree, Mattie, a little mom and pop stuff never hurt anything."

"I've read some things lately about market socialism. It seemed to make some sense."

"Uh-huh, some."

"Maybe if they'd allowed more of that things wouldn't have gotten so out of hand that they fell apart."

"Could be, but I think, or I am afraid, that they've fallen for the full 'free market' routine, and that instead of it being the salvation they think it'll be, their societies will just turn into inequitable capitalist crapholes."

Duane came back into the room. "What craphole is that?" He handed a cold beer to Frank and this time pulled a chair up alongside Mattie's end of the couch.

"Yugoslavia." Frank pointed at the TV even though a commercial was on. "It used to be the shining star of socialism—not to be confused with communism, of course—but what about now? In the toilet, and they even allowed small businesses there. It just went blooey."

"You still have that rap down, don't you, bud?" Duane raised his beer in salute. Frank followed suit.

"Primitive accumulation of capital, dialectical materialism, profit is surplus value is—"

"The difference between the cost of producing a commodity and the price charged for it." Duane finished. "Is this ranting and raving, or what?" He got up and plopped down on the couch beside Mattie. He put his arm around her and hugged her.

"Definitely ranting and raving." She hugged him back.

"It's good having you visit again." Duane told Frank. "I haven't heard that old political stuff in a long time."

"I do have the buzzwords down, huh?"

"Well, now that you've both got that out of your systems." Mattie suggested. "How's about some plain old non-political TV?"

"Cool by me."

"Go for it." Duane handed Mattie the remote control and she surfed through the numerous cable channels, stopping at one that played middle of the road pop and rock.

"This okay?"

"Don't matter to me." Frank told her.

"That's fine." Duane took a drink of beer. "Makes okay background noise."

They were silent for a while, checking out the various videos of middle-aged sixties rockers and contemporary artists whose claim to fame seemed to be an unwillingness to produce anything that was challenging or interesting.

"Boring, huh?" Frank commented after a particularly puerile video. "Fifty-seven channels and nothing on TV."

"Let's kill it." Mattie shut off the TV with the press of a fingertip. "We have to get up early tomorrow and work around the house."

Frank stood.

"You want to help us, bud?" Duane asked.

"Gotta repay you for supper, don't I?"

"Absolutely." Duane rose and stretched.

"Time to hit the hay." Mattie stood by his side.

Duane put his arm around her waist, and they walked out of the family room side by side, legs bumping together.

"Beddy-bye time." Frank followed, happy to be with old friends once again.

They passed out of the family room into the outer hallway. Frank paused at the doorway. "Goodnight, John Boy."

He flipped the light switch and giggled at his little joke.

16

YOU GUYS SEEM TO HAVE really found it here." The friends weeded out the big vegetable garden. "Happiness, contentment, whatever 'it' is."

In the shade of two large oak trees growing alongside the house, the kids played a game of keep away with a ball they tossed back and forth over the head of the good-natured and apparently not too bright Biff. The big dog never tired of the game, and if the kids lagged in their duties, he barked and wagged his tail in a spasm of hopefulness.

Mattie paused in her work. "We didn't so much find it as it found us."

"It wasn't a matter of trying to be happy." Duane elaborated. "You can't really do that, but it can come to you, or you can become it. You can't strive for it and get it."

"Sounds zen."

"Yeah, but I believe it, anyway."

"I think I do, too, actually." Frank went back to the weeding.

"It might sound hokey." Mattie wiped a trickle of sweat off her cheek. "But living here on the farm, we feel the heat, the cold, the wind, and rain. We can see the stars at night. Our schedule at MU is perfect: we teach on alternating days so whoever's home works on whatever needs to be done here. On the weekends, we go hiking or camping with the kids. All in all we feel in tune with the land and with the seasons. It's a satisfying life."

"Except for my back." Frank straightened up and massaged his muscles. "It doesn't like this at all."

"Take your time," Duane told him. "There's no hurry on this stuff."

"Everything in its own time."

"Exactly."

"But what about the future?"

"What about it?"

"Do you plan for it?"

"Yes, but we don't obsess on it. Our idea of looking ahead is to think about where we might go during the next summer break."

"I wish I could be like that. I always seem to be out of synch. I'm either living or reliving the past, or I'm projecting into the future. Remember talking about what we were going to be back in school days, Duane?"

"Sure. That's what young guys in transition do. But, you know, what I think it's all about is in the day-to-day living. Being satisfied with the doing of life, with the process, not with the trying to attain something. Goals are all right, but they're not the end all. Enjoying the getting there, that's the secret."

"Right on, but that ain't an easy thing to do."

"No, we're too western. We have to always 'go for it,' never just let it happen."

"Exactly. Jake and I had a similar talk when I visited him just lately."

"He still farming the magic herb?"

"Uh-huh. He said to tell you all hello."

"Do the same for us when you see him again."

"Sure."

For the better part of an hour, the conversation was put on hold as the group concentrated on weeding Finally, Duane stood up, stretched his back, and called for a water break. He hollered at the kids, and they came running over with a big water jug, Biff racing along happily at their side. The adults drank greedily, Frank letting the water pour out of his mouth, down his chin, and onto his sweaty T-shirt. The kids giggled at him, and he grabbed at them. They ran away squealing, Biff again trailing along.

"You know, guys. I was thinking—"

"Very dangerous for you." Duane teased.

"Meany." Mattie pretended to hit him.

"Just telling the truth."

"Go on. What were you going to say?"

"Oh, I was just considering how you all live and how I do. It's peculiar, but all my life I've thought of myself as being out of rhythm with things, like I was living behind time somehow, a Johnny-Come-Lately to ideas, movements, careers, you name it. Always one, two, even five or ten years behind what's happening."

"You're not being fair to yourself, Frank. You've been hip to everything since I've known you. Maybe instead of behind, you're ahead of time."

"Maybe, but I've never felt that way. Look at me now. I've tuned in, turned on, and dropped out. Twenty-five years after the fact."

"But for you it's not behind time." Duane drew a circle in the air. "You've come back around. You're being who you were back then, again."

"I've always felt I was born a little too early to be at the true heart of our age. That sort of belongs to the boomers, you know. I'm not as confident as they seem to be, so I've always been reticent about getting involved in things."

"Some people might call that common sense." Duane suggested.

"Or being maladjusted, or chicken or whatever. Either way I've missed a lot because I've been out of synch so often. For somebody who's been around as long as I have, there are some basic realities I just never learned to deal with."

"Well—"

"I don't mean to whine. I'm just describing the way it is as I see it."

Mattie put her hand on Frank's arm. "We love you just the way you are."

"Don't be condescending, Mattie. Frank's a big boy now. He can handle life okay."

"I didn't mean it to sound that way."

"Don't worry about it. I know what you mean, and I appreciate it. I love you guys, too. And you seem to have found it here, whatever it is. I'm envious."

"There's always a place for you here, Frank." Duane offered. "You can see we have the room."

"The door's always open." Mattie patted his hand.

"Thanks, you all are tops. Maybe when I get to wherever it is I'm going I'll come back and take you up on it. Be your neighbor or something, though."

Mattie wrapped her arm around Frank's waist. "Do you have to go already?"

"There's a lot more of this garden work yet to do." Duane kidded.

"That's why I'm moving on."

"The kids adore you." Mattie held onto his arm.

"I love them, too. All of you. But I have to go on for now. This is your life here. Mine might be something like it, or maybe not. I'll have to find out on my own."

"We'll be here if you need us."

"I appreciate that, Duane."

"Don't stay gone so long, okay?" Mattie teared up. "We miss you terribly."

"Let's fart this garden off and go have a beer, what do you say?"

"You're an idea man, bud. Most excellent."

"And there's one more thing we have to do before you boogie."

The kids and Biff came racing toward the grownups. Biff crashed against Mattie's legs, nearly knocking her over, and the kids stormed Frank, one grabbing each arm and pulling him toward the house.

"What's that, man?"

"Columbia, we gotta do Columbia."

"Right on." Frank called back over his shoulder.

"Do it first thing in the morning. You can split from there."

Frank couldn't answer this time. The kids were dragging him pall mall into the backyard, all three of them whooping like wild banshees.

17

W E'RE A LONG WAY FROM old West Central College, huh, Frankie?" They walked along the sidewalk in front of Jesse Hall on the University of Missouri campus.

"Only about a million years."

"And, what, around a hundred fifty miles as the crow flies?"

"At least that far and those days might as well have happened on Mars for all I can see that remains of them."

"Columbia's still a decent place, though."

"Yeah, well, MU and Columbia were always a hell of a lot cooler places than WCC and Lewisburg. Not a fair comparison."

"No, it's not."

"The coeds here still as pretty as in the old days?"

"If you allow for the new hair and clothes styles, yep, they sure are."

"And the pretty ones in your classes always get the best grades."

"That's how it works."

"You keeping your filthy mitts off of 'em?"

Duane led the way down the sidewalk leading to Jesse Hall. "Best I can."

"Best you can? You're not doing one now?"

"Not now."

"You bastard, pokin' some babe-o-rama coed and not comin' clean with old Frankie?"

"I'm not pokin' anybody."

"Oh, wrong tense, were pokin'. Excuse me. Who was it and when?"

"It—she—was a graduate student, six or seven years ago."

Frank whistled. "Does Mattie know?"

"I think she suspected at the time." They approached the entrance to Jesse Hall. "But it's been so long now it's all ancient history."

"I can't believe you'd want anybody but Mattie." They paused in front of the building.

"Hell, it was a long time ago. We were in a bad place in our marriage. It just happened. I suppose you're gonna tell me you were true blue in your marriage?"

"Not because I wanted to be. I guess I was always too chicken."

"You never did it with anybody else?"

"Oh, I wanted to. Half-tried a couple of times and did do some cheap feeling now and then, but that was it."

"I'll be damned."

"But you, hell, you screwed around on one of the best women in the country, man."

"Don't get sanctimonious on me, bud. I told you it was a one-time deal. It's long over now. Give me a break."

"Yeah, you're right. Sorry."

"Listen, Frankie, I gotta run in here and take care of some business. Then we'll get a sandwich and something to drink around the corner at one of the joints, okay? I won't be long."

"I'll walk around some and reminisce. I haven't been here in a lot of years."

"Be back soon as I can." Duane hurried inside Jesse Hall.

Frank stood out in front of the building for a few moments thinking about Duane's confession. He had been acting sanctimonious with him. Hell, just because he'd always had a crush on Mattie didn't mean that if he had her he wouldn't do the same thing.

Relationships only seemed to last about seven or eight years, anyway, at least most of them. Then it was all familiarity and the old saw about it breeding contempt. After that, both partners were usually seeking something more satisfying. Usually it broke up a relationship, but maybe Duane's fling with the graduate student had somehow helped his and Mattie's marriage. They seemed happy now. And that was all that counted. How things were now.

Without realizing it, he had walked back out to the road and walked up Conley Street to the left. The day, which had started warm and sunny, had turned cooler, and clouds were rolling in. It reminded him of the old saying about Missouri weather. If you don't like it, wait five minutes. It'll change. Smiling, he walked along, letting the sights and sounds of the MU campus bring back a freight-train load of old memories. He took a deep breath as if to inhale the past.

He remembered coming down here to see his old friend Brad Owens after he had been booted out of WCC. Brad had been set up, arrested, tried, and luckily acquitted. But WCC and the local authorities had driven him from Lewisburg to seek asylum in the friendlier surroundings of MU and Columbia. Frank, Duane, and some others had visited their friend in Columbia, trying to cheer him up. All that seemed so distant now, yet occasionally he could bring back flashes or sounds or smells of that time for just a moment.

Oh, how he missed those days sometimes. Maybe it was just his youth he longed for, but the tug of the era was equally strong, and he knew in his heart it was both.

And then he remembered Everyday People. He couldn't exactly place where the old crash pad house had been, but it seemed like it was not too far from where he was, at least somewhere close to the campus, somewhere nearby. It had been a long time. He did remember going there once.

Freaks were always welcome. It was one of those classic Victorian houses with almost no furniture and an atmosphere blending strangeness and togetherness all at once, wood floors and sleeping bags all over the place. It was dirty and smelled, but it was a place to stay if you were on the road. And in those days, lots of people were on the road. He gave himself over to a wave of sights and sounds from many years before. The memories rushed to him, filled him, reverberated through him. He felt the thread of still living history, felt himself linked to that thread.

He walked along, no longer paying attention to his surroundings. History does reverberate through time, especially the history of a special time you were a part of, like the 60s. It was cool to trash that era now, but it had been alive in a way that no other period since could even vaguely attempt to match.

"The days that used to be." He recalled Neil Young's plaintive ballad of lost youth and promise. No wonder people got stuck in a particular time. Especially if that time happened to coincide with their own youth and strength and if it also happened to be one of those infrequent cycles of considerable historical import. It was no marvel that many people found it difficult to come out of a specific time or that they might wallow in so much nostalgic retrospection, just as their folks did with the 30s and 40s. Those were, as the worn out phrase went, the good old days.

He stopped on the lawn above Jesse Hall and scanned the campus without really seeing it. The past, no matter how appealing it still seems, is still the past—you had to move on, make the best of where you were at any given time. And even if it did seem unlikely that you could possibly live through two significant historical periods in one lifetime, which he seriously doubted, if you chose to live, you had to go on living in time, in the present.

You didn't forget the past, but you had to get beyond it. You had to try to reach some sort of accommodation with your present. He approached Jesse Hall and saw Duane coming out, knowing that they would soon be saying goodbye and that his journey would go on from Columbia. He realized with the power of a drug-induced high that now, right now, this instant—which is always becoming the next instant—is the only reality there is.

Every person alive at any given moment, is always at the edge of existence, at the border of time, borne along unrelentingly by unceasing, perpetually moving time. Hurtling forward without cessation, without recourse, at the tip of time's speeding, unstoppable arrow.

"Are you ready to go?" Duane broke into his thoughts.

He exhaled and brought himself back to the physical reality around him. He felt like he'd just come down from being high.

"Yes." His own voice sounded distant to him and a series of vague images of the highway and where it might be leading him flashed through his mind's eye. "I'm ready to go."

18

HELLO. THIS IS KIM ADAMS." The voice Frank heard on the other end of the phone was rich, smooth and confident. He remembered it well, remembered the first time he'd heard it— five summers ago when he'd helped organize a shipment of humanitarian aid to Nicaragua. He'd been approached by a young TV reporter who wanted a talking head for the 10 o'clock news.

Despite his knee-jerk antipathy to mainstream journalists, the young reporter had easily won him over and gotten the ten-second blurb she wanted. That beautiful voice, deeper than normal, a little husky, was as much responsible as her appearance.

"No, it's not." He tried to sound unfriendly, even a little hostile.

"*Pardon me?*"

"No way are you *the* Kim Adams." He softened his tone slightly. "I believe that's nothing more than a cover for some nefarious ne'er-do-well escapee from La Jolla and the CHP."

"*Frankie.*" Her tone mixed recognition with amusement. "*Is it you?*"

"That's right, Little Ms. Memphis Eyewitless News Weekend Anchor Kim Adams, nee Ellen Marie Gillespie of Dubuque, Iowa, it's me, Frank."

"*You old fart, I'm so happy to hear from you. How are you?*"

He pictured her as he'd last seen her, wearing her short, boyish hair in a stylish feminine wave with little or no makeup to mar her well-tanned outdoor girl face. The solid, athletic body, with muscular legs he could still see always jogging several strides ahead of his. He hoped she hadn't changed much. "How you been?"

"*Things are going well. 'Eyewitless News,' as you call it is treating me well. I have no complaints.*"

"That's good."

"*Where are you, Frankie?*" He had been saving his surprise, holding it until he was more certain of revealing it. "*You still out in San Diego?*"

"As a matter of fact, I'm just across the bridge—or I should say *bridges*—in the cultural mecca of the New South, West Memphis, AR, as in Arkansas."

"*West Memphis! How in the world did you get there?*"

"Well, let's see. I went toward St. Louis, then down through the Boot Heel, past—"

"*You know what I mean, you stupid nut.*"

"I'm just sort of traveling around. Visiting friends and places I haven't seen in a while."

"*Doing a Kerouac-Kesey kind of thing?*"

"I don't think so, unless old, unhip, single, and unemployed can substitute for young, hip, single, and so on. At least I got part of it right."

There was a pause on the other end of the line. "*What did you do?*"

"I quit my job. I took what little I had left, put it in storage, and took off."

"*Whew.*" She whistled. "*Broke right out of there, huh?*"

"Just let it go."

"*That's a really brave thing to do.*"

"Or stupid. The verdict is still out."

"*Amazing, my Frankie just cutting loose. I don't know what to make of it.*"

"Me, either."

"*Were you coming down here to see me?*"

"I wish I could say yes, but it was really just a lucky break. I was heading for Biloxi and decided to stop here for the night. Next thing I know I'm scanning the TV news in my motel room, and the reporter babe comes on, and I say, "Whoa, I gotta call this momma up!"

"Frank, you are such a dork."

"It was completely by accident. I wasn't sure you were still in Memphis, but I'm really happy I got hold of you."

"Me, too."

He pictured her serious green eyes, her thin nose with the two little freckles up by the bridge, her firm perfect mouth always ready to form into a wry smile. He barely restrained what would have been an audible sigh. Crossing his fingers, he plunged forward to where he hoped he would get from the moment he'd seen her on the TV in his downscale motel room. "So, uh, what do you think, any chance we can get together? If you can spare the time."

"You are truly a ding-dong. This is Kim you're talking to. We've been around a couple of blocks together in case you've forgotten."

"I haven't forgotten, I'm sorry. It's been a while—no? I didn't know how things were with you. You never know about that."

"Well, get this straight, traveling boy, you know I'll always have time for you. We're friends, too, aren't we?"

"Yeah." He let out a deep breath. "I know but—"

"But what?"

"Maybe you got married or something. Are you?"

"Just to my job."

"Same old Kim."

"Same old."

"So—" He started.

"So let's get together." She finished.

"Couldn't make me happier."

"Want me to come get you, or do you think you can find downtown?"

"I can try to find it. It's been a long time, but I'll get directions."

"It's fairly easy. I can give them to you. We'll do a late night out. I know a little place off Beale Street. You'll love it."

"Just a second." He dug through his day bag for a pencil and piece of paper. The pack of Marlboros fell out onto the bed. "Good Lord." He put them back in the pack, "I didn't know I still had those."

"What?"

"Nothing." He pulled out writing materials from an internal pocket. "Just saw something I forgot I had. Okay, I got my writing implements. Lay the directions on me."

19

FRANK MANAGED TO GET DOWNTOWN on I-40 but got lost a couple of times on 2nd and 3rd streets before he found the New Mississippi Hotel where Kim had told him to meet her. She was waiting for him in the lobby, standing to one side of the check-in counter browsing a USA Today. If anything, his recollection was a slight to her. She was as beautiful as ever, maybe even more so than he had remembered from San Diego days.

She stood with one hip jutted casually out, giving her an air of unselfconscious sexuality, wearing expensive running shoes and a light blue, short-sleeved work shirt tucked into her form-fitting dark jeans. Her hair was longer now than in the past, almost shoulder length, and was full and shaggy. Seeing her like that, with her not yet aware of him, made him feel as if he might die of longing on the spot.

"Frank." She tossed down the paper and came toward him with her arms outstretched.

"Hi, Kimmie." He took her into his arms in a firm and solid warm hug. "It's been a long time."

They hugged each other for a long moment, then she leaned back, holding onto his arms, and gave him the once-over.

"Not too much worse for the wear just a touch of dignified gray."

"Oh, well, a little touch of gray kind of suits me, anyway."

"The Dead."

"The Dead. And you—you're prettier than ever."

"You're sweet." She put her right arm around his waist. "I'm so glad to see you again. Sorry we lost touch."

"Well, I've found you again, now." He gazed into those bright, intelligent eyes. "I won't let you escape again so easily."

She squeezed his side, but didn't say anything. He fought against but couldn't stop a road-induced urge to yawn. He tried to cover it with a little cough, but she saw through his minor subterfuge.

"Are you up to doing this, or are you too tired? We could do something else or call it off."

"No way." He was not the least bit willing to part from her after this serendipitous reunion. "Lead on McDuff—or Lady McDuff, or whatever."

"Okay, let's go listen to some real blues. You'll love the place."

"Let's do it." He let her pull him along by the hand. "I'm your man."

The Blues Off Beale Club was a surprise. He had expected a renovated, regenerated, yuppie bar with some pseudo-blues band cranking out refried rock and roll. What he found instead was an actual, funky, smoky, noisy, mixed crowd blues bar. Up on the bandstand, a shriveled little man who might have stepped out of a 1920s Arkansas Delta cotton field banged on a worn out old guitar, groaning through a handful of bad teeth the best blues he had ever heard live.

Kim directed him toward a table near a side wall across the room from the bandstand, and they found chairs at the edge of the group occupying the table, people that he assumed to be journalist friends of hers. Besides her yuppy friends, the place had a refreshing mix of people, blending post-punks and post-freaks with upscale blacks, wild eyed musicians, and blue collar whites and blacks into a fascinating music appreciation melting pot.

A completely disinterested waitress dropped by for their order and shortly brought them back ice cold beers and soiled beer glasses. Kim wiped hers off with a napkin, but Frank drank from the bottle while settling back to listen to the music.

"Terrific place, huh?" She asked between songs.

"Outstanding."

She tried to introduce some of the people at the table, but the little old singer launched into another number.

"Frank." She got his attention after he had joined the general hooting and hollering for the little blues man when his song ended. "I want you to meet some other folks from the station."

"Uh-huh." He wasn't totally keen on being introduced to what he took to be a gaggle of self-important mainstream TV people.

If he hadn't been with Kim, he would have rather been at any of the other tables in the bar than the one they were. Her friends were too clean, too shiny, too Goddamned concerned about the roles they played in their little community for his taste. But that was exactly the opinion he'd had of her when he first saw her in San Diego and now he thought she was one of the coolest people he'd known. But maybe that was just hormones, even adult ones, doing the evaluating for him.

She pointed to a heavy-set lady to her immediate right. "This is Patti Jones. She's one of our producers. And Bill Torrance, our early afternoon co-anchor."

"Hello."

Frank pointed an index finger at Bill, noting that the co-anchor's hairpiece was of cheaper manufacture than one would expect in a midsize market like Memphis.

"Next to Bill is Gina Carrow. Gina just joined us a couple of months ago. She's doing general assignments now, but we have high hopes for her."

"How are you, Gina?"

She was maybe twenty-three or twenty-four at the most, tall and slender, with hair a shade or two darker than her smooth brown skin. She would go places if she could speak at all.

"I suppose the first assignment they gave you was to cover them digging up the king?"

"The king?"

"The Elvii. The King. Little Elvis. Big Elvis. Old, young, everywhere Elvis."

"Thank the Lord, no." Gina giggled. "I'm not ready for that yet."

"I'm surprised you haven't come up with an angle of your own. It's your sure fire ticket to the top."

"And last but not least." Kim interrupted Frank with a little kick to the shins under the table. "Next to Gina is Peter Conway, our international reporter."

He reluctantly shifted his attention from Gina and fixed it on the man. Peter was handsome and clean, shiny, scrubbed, well groomed, with a fraternity boy look that to Frank suggested uncalled-for self-importance. He seemed like the kind of guy who would never have self-doubts, not because he was so skilled at what he did, but because he was too egocentric to consider his own actions as anything other than the correct ones. Frank also forced himself to admit that he mostly saw Peter as his rival for Kim and to remember that his first impressions of people were almost always wrong.

"Hi." He hoped he sounded open and friendly.

Peter barely acknowledged him with a brief glance. Frank gleefully prepared to say the first rude thing about reporters he could think of, but Kim spoke right through the verbal space he was planning to fill.

"Peter covered the Gulf War for us. We're really proud of him."

He slowly released his breath. Joe Cool is a frappin' war correspondent hero.

"Is that right?" He tried to sound impressed.

At least Kim's flattery had gotten Peter's attention. He now seemed to notice the others at the table for the first time, as if they had been dropped down beside him from somewhere in outer space.

"It was a challenging experience." Peter might as well have been reading a teleprompter. Frank glanced over at Patti and Bill, who were whispering something to each other. "It was a stretch for us."

"How long were you there?"

"Eight days."

"Eight days? That must have been challenging. Were you there for the ground war?"

"No." Peter reluctantly admitted, for the first time acknowledging Frank's existence—also reluctantly, it seemed.

"Peter was in Riyadh when some of the missiles hit." Gina pointed out.

"That's right." Kim confirmed. "Very scary."

Patti and Bill unobtrusively slipped out of their seats and headed to the front of the club and its short, rectangle of a bar. Kim and Gina winked at each other.

"Did you meet Charles Jaeckel over there?" Frank hoped to annoy Peter with his questions. "Now that's a professional reporter. He was scared shitless over there on the first nights they started flinging SCUDs all over the place."

"Sure, I knew Charlie over there. We used to have a drink or two together."

"So tell me, Peter, how did you like being part of the most manipulated and managed press corps in the history of the U.S. 'free' press? You guys really rolled over and played dead for that one, didn't you?"

Kim sighed. Gina snickered. Peter smirked.

"You would have had to have been there. Not many people know what it was really like."

"I'm sure. As far as I could tell, there wasn't anything reported except what you people got from the military or—"

"Hey, Willie's going to sing again." Kim broke in as the little blues man began to check the tuning on his guitar and to strum it.

Frank acted like he didn't hear, so she put her left arm around his shoulders and turned him to face the singer.

"Over there."

"All right." He scooted his chair closer to hers. "Let's crank it out."

Across the table, Peter resumed his unconcerned attitude, but added a final rejoinder. "They know a lot more about things than we do. That's why they're in charge, and people who don't know anything aren't."

Frank turned back to face him, ready to counter that pathetic old saw, but Kim was right on him. She rubbed his shoulders and patted him on the hands. Peter stared off into the bar as if he might be doing a visual sizing of the hole in the ozone. Frank settled for a hostile glare that was ignored or not seen. Gina watched Frank with laughter in her eyes. He glanced over at her and winked. She winked back.

Kim leaned against him so he could feel the warm firmness of her breasts. "Stop flirting with my friend."

He looked into those playful, light emerald eyes and grinned. He didn't really care about guys like Peter. It was just residual political behavior from the old days when you argued about everything with everybody. He let what was left of his mini-flareup flow out of him with a slow release of breath and took Kim's hand in his. She did not resist.

"I'm glad to be back in Memphis, seeing you again."

"I'm really glad you came." She whispered in his ear.

Patti and Bill rejoined the group as Willie prepared to play again. They nodded for Gina to check out Kim and Frank. Peter continued to stare out at the bar as if he were in the place alone. Willie broke into a spirited version of Robert Johnson's "Ramblin.'"

With Kim pressing close against him, Frank leaned back in his chair, stretched his legs out on the dirty floor, and settled in to enjoy the music.

20

MEMPHIS, TENNESSEE—1970

SHERRY WAITRESSED IN A MEXICAN restaurant in West Memphis where Frank had found a job as DJ in the back bar and disco. She was tall and bleach-blonde with a body that would someday go to fat, but was as yet soft and voluptuous. Working together nights, they developed an easy-going friendship that soon developed into a sexually-charged flirtation.

"Hey, Sherry." He called down from his DJ's booth above and to the right of the bandstand and the dance floor.

He had twin turntables in the booth on which he spun a mix of Top-40 forty-fives mostly—the boss frowned on his forays into long, psychedelic LP cuts. And he ran the light show, such as it was, mostly flashing colored lights for fast songs and turning on the spinning, obligatory mirror ball for slow ones.

"Would you bring me a hamburger, fries, and a coke when you get a chance?"

"Just a sec, baby." Sherry mouthed to him from below.

He gave her the high sign and went back to his seat between the turntables. It was still early on a weeknight with few people back in the bar so he debated on whether to play Hendrix's "Third Stone from the Sun" or "Lodi" by CCR. He was about to put on Hendrix when Chuck the boss drifted in from the restaurant up front, so Frank did a musical about face and put on the Temptations doing "Ball of Confusion." Four songs later he was playing "1-2-3" when Sherry popped into the booth with his food.

"Here you go, sugar." She set the food on the counter just inside the door.

"Thanks." He turned to admire her long fine legs, her full rump, and solid breasts. She wore no bra under a practically sheer, light blue blouse, and when she flipped her long hair out of the way, her nipples rigidly thrust out against the blouse. "Put it on my tab?"

"I did better than that." She leaned sexily against the side of his booth. "I put it on Chuck's tab."

"You didn't?" He forced his gaze from her full breasts to her full mouth.

"Uh-huh." She ran her moist tongue over inviting lips.

He took a deep breath and with a considerable act of discipline turned from the young waitress to his food.

"Why do you always get hamburgers here?" She asked as he opened a catsup container and squeezed some on his fries. "We're a Mexican food restaurant. Don't you like Mexican food?"

He chewed a particularly large fry. "Oh, I love Mexican food. I just like burgers, too."

He wiped his hands, started the second turntable with "Hitchin' a Ride" and switched the new song onto the room speakers.

"I gotta go back down, baby." Her voice made his groin ache. "Chuck could come out and give me some shit."

"Okay, thanks for the food. It was real sweet of you."

She winked and turned to go, then stopped. "Say, you wanna go into Memphis with me and Roger sometime? We're gonna check out some record stores. We'll be back in time for work."

"Who's Roger?"

"A friend of mine."

"A friend?"

"Yeah, that's all. Just a dude. C'mon, it'll be groovy."

"Groovy, huh? Sounds heavy to me."

"Stop that. You know what I mean."

He thought about this unknown Roger guy and what a drag he might be, then he thought about spending most of the day with Sherry. No contest.

"I'm your man."

She winked again and hurried back down to the bar. He enjoyed every bit of her walk as she went back to work.

The following Saturday, they went to two or three different record stores in Memphis, and he felt like an unhip third wheel the entire time. He dug Leonard Cohen, Joe Cocker, and Hendrix, while Sherry and Roger were into Delta blues and Motown. Although there was no reason for it, he felt like his musical tastes were outdated and somehow uncool. Mostly they hung together with him on the outside.

When they got back to West Memphis, they all went to her place and toked up. He felt better after that, and some heat generated between him and Sherry, but the Roger guy wouldn't leave them alone for more than a couple of minutes at a time. Once when Roger went out of the living room for a beer, Frank managed a quick kiss and a furtive hand against her breast, but they had to separate hurriedly when he came thudding back in. Eventually it was time to go to work, and they dropped Frank off, spaced out and sexually frustrated, at his place.

That night at work, they picked up their ritual flirtation as usual, but they never got together again during the short Arkansas summer. Three weeks later, he headed back up to Missouri for the fall semester and Sherry, though not easily forgotten, became just another memory of his youth and of things that might have been but never were.

21

FRANK WOKE UP ON KIM'S couch with a road and alcohol hangover and the sinking feeling he might be in her doghouse. Rising gingerly and cradling his head, he found a bathroom and splashed some cold water on his face. By the time he came out, feeling more alert than when he went in, he was surprised to hear her singing and, from the sound of pots and pans being moved around in the kitchen, making breakfast.

"Good morning, handsome." She greeted him when he came into the kitchen-dining room of her split level condominium in an upscale area of suburban, white flight Germantown.

He was at least fully awake now, if not energetic. He took her in, standing by the stove. She wore jogging shoes and shorts and a soft gray, cotton T-shirt that made his heart ache.

"Hi."

"Would you like some pancakes?" She poured out a bubbly white mixture onto a hot griddle.

He walked up next to her and checked out a cooling stack of pancakes on a plate by the stove. She winked at him. He gave her what he hoped was a not inappropriate kiss on the cheek. She didn't seem to be offended by it.

"I could do one or two and some OJ. Got any?"

"In the fridge." She pointed to her right. "Me, too."

He found the juice, poured them each a glass, and placed them on the small dining table across from the stove.

"Sit down." She brought him a plate with two steaming, browned pancakes.

What couldn't this woman do? He dutifully sat down, facing the stove so he could see her.

"Come join me." He vainly tried to stem the flood of affection that seeing her again had unleashed within him.

"Be right there." She popped a couple of the cooling pancakes into a microwave built into the cabinet above and to the left of the stove. In a few seconds they were ready and she settled in at the table. "I want to thank you."

"For what? I expect I owe you an apology for being so rude to your friends."

"Except for Gina, they're not really my friends, and you just flirted with her. You weren't rude."

"I was thinking of that Peter guy."

"That's what I meant. Thanks for not fighting with him. I know where you're coming from about journalism, but he doesn't have a clue."

"He does seem to be full of himself." Frank chuckled between bites.

"It's an occupational hazard. A lot of people think of us as celebrities, including us. It can go to your head."

"I think it's too late for him."

"Well, despite the attitude, he doesn't really have a lot of experience yet. But he's not a bad guy, once you get to know him."

"I suppose." Frank sought neutrality.

For a moment or two they concentrated on their food, eating in silence, a silence he finally had to break.

He hid behind his orange juice glass.

"Do you know him really well?"

She shrugged. "We work together. What do you mean, exactly?"

"You know."

"No, I don't know."

"Are you seeing each other?"

"No."

"Hmm."

"We went out a couple of times but it never went anywhere. There was nothing there, nothing to it. If it's any of your business."

"Oh, I'm sorry."

"I was only kidding. You through?"

"Huh? Oh, yeah."

He handed her his dirty dishes. She put hers on top of his and took them over to the sink. She glanced over her shoulder at him while she rinsed the dishes and put them in the dishwasher.

"You're not jealous of Peter, are you?"

"No, no. Um, well, maybe, sort of. Yes."

"I like that, a man who knows his own mind, a decisive man."

"Well, hell, I feel like a teeny bopper with his first crush."

"That's honest." She dried her hands on a dish towel.

"I make no claims for myself. Right now, I'm just sort of free floating."

"Bed and breakfasting America with your friends?"

"Yes. And thank you for both. That was a big breakfast and thanks for cleaning up, too."

"I don't mind doing it, sometimes. As long as no one gets to expecting it. I wouldn't cotton to that much."

"Cotton to?" He smirked. "Man, you have been down here too long already. Time to vacate for a more northerly position in a larger market."

"You know what I meant, smart alec."

"Yes, I do and I never take help from others for granted. Anything given to you by anybody is strictly from the kindness of their hearts. The way I figure it, a person deserves nothing, and no one owes them anything. Everything you are given or receive is in the nature of a gift."

"That's an interesting attitude. A little too binary for me."

"I'm a binary thinker. Not too creative, but useful when you're trying to be self-sufficient."

"Is that what's behind this trip, some kind of need to be self-sufficient?"

"To tell you the truth, I don't really know. I just took off from San Diego, and I've been moving ever since. I don't know what would happen if I stopped."

"Maybe if you stopped somewhere long enough, you'd find yourself. Who you are would come to you."

"That's possible."

"It's all in there, Frankie." She pointed at his chest. "You have to change what's inside. What's outside is out of your control."

"I've been told that." He thought of his recent visits in Missouri. "But not so precisely. You're a sharp cookie—for a TV reporter babe."

She swatted him across his left bicep with her open right hand. He acted intimidated.

"Yeah, well, this TV reporter babe is free until mid-afternoon. What would the traveling boy like to do today? A little sightseeing of the new Memphis? Old Memphis?"

"Anywhere you want to take me—except to Graceland. I'd rather leave the king in peace."

"We will not bother the king." She crossed her heart. "I promise you that."

"It would grieve me to think that my disbelieving presence might disturb the king's eternal rest. Grieve me sorely."

"I can see that." She collected her purse and keys off a coffee table as they walked out into the living room. "I can see that plain as day."

———

KIM TOOK HIM AROUND TO some of the parts of town he remembered, by Memphis State and then Christian Brothers where he'd gone to a CBC-Southern Illinois baseball game on a visit to his sister Kathy's a couple of years before he worked in West Memphis. They drove by the Liberty Bowl and then to the zoo where they spent most of their time. He enjoyed exchanging glares with a baboon that stared at him as though he was as smart as Frank.

They went downtown to the Mid America Mall, a quick tour since he wasn't much up for it, and finally found themselves at a quiet restaurant-lounge with an excellent view of the Mississippi, Mud Island, and the Pyramid. Though he knew little of Mud Island and was fascinated by the glass and steel of the Pyramid, it was the sight of the second bridge that most occupied his attention.

He had left West Memphis apparently just before it had been built. To

Memphians it was already an old sight, but to Frank it was the "new" bridge. Off to his left, he was comforted by the sight of the old bridge in the distance.

"Penny for your thoughts." Kim broke into his reflections. He focused on her face and lied, though saying the lie out loud made it true.

"I was thinking how lucky I am to be right here, right now, with you."

"Why didn't we ever get together, Frank?" She sipped on a glass of house chardonnay and gazed at him seriously.

He slowly turned a light beer in his hand. "I was married?"

"Or was that just an excuse?"

He didn't have an answer for that one.

"I'm sorry, that wasn't fair."

"There is no such thing as fair. I just don't know what to say. Do you think we could get together? Is it possible with us?"

"Anything's possible."

"A man would have to be a fool not to consider that possibility with you."

"It's not easy, though, being involved with journalists. Of all people, you should know that."

"Yeah."

"And I know your general opinion of the field and the people in it. I know you don't hold us in high regard."

"I don't hold the system in high regard. And the media is part of that. It's the mouthpiece. It can point out things that are not right within, but it can never challenge the system itself. In that sense it's just as big a dupe as the state-controlled presses we used to scream about in the former commie world."

She frowned. "I don't think I like being called a dupe."

"Present company excepted. I see the system as flawed, but there are decent people within it. Sincere people trying to get it to work as advertised."

"Is that how you see yourself in computers?"

"Not anymore. I'm a dropout. I no longer lay any claims to being, if I ever actually was, a useful member of society."

"I don't buy that." She laid her left hand on his right forearm. He put his left hand on top of hers, and they interlaced fingers.

"You shouldn't. I ramble on too much and say nothing. I'm completely full of it. You know. . . ." He took her hand in both of his and gazed into her eyes.

"In a moment of lucidity a couple of years ago it occurred to me that at least in my case, speech was my enemy. If I spoke less, I would be a lot better off. Real wisdom, I realized, is silence."

"That would be a fine philosophy, if you were a Tibetan monk lost in the Himalayas. It's a little hard to follow here in the old U. S. of A."

"Like I said, I'm full of it."

She took her hand from between his to check her watch. "Even if you are, I still like you. A lot."

"You gotta go?"

"We better. I've got to run you out to my place and come back down here."

"I'm sorry. I wasn't even thinking about that. I should have driven my car."

"No, no, I was planning on this. It's not a problem."

"Well, thanks for an outstanding day." He dropped a couple of bills on the table for a tip.

She stood. "You're perfectly welcome. I'm really happy you came."

"Likewise, and I really like you a lot, too."

She put her arm around his waist, and they walked toward the lounge exit.

They approached the double doors. "By the way, what were you really thinking about a while ago when I asked you about it?"

"A penny for my thoughts?"

"Yeah."

"I was just thinking of the old days."

"Of course." She did not loosen her hold around his waist.

He reached over and hugged her. "You're such a special woman. She leaned forward and kissed him on the mouth.

"Wait up for me? I'll be late, but try, okay?"

"Don't you worry, I'll be there when you come in. You can bank on that."

22

FRANK WAS DOZING ON THE living room couch, the TV tuned to some long forgotten 40s B-movie when Kim came in from work. She quietly closed the door, set her things down, and tiptoed over to the side of the couch. Observing him like that, his head lolled to one side, his thinning gray hair messed up, the onset of middle age beginning to alter his features, she wondered why she cared as much about him as she felt she did. He was average in most ways except for perhaps a more inquisitive mind than normal, and he hadn't accomplished much with his life.

Traveling around in a beat up old Toyota, living out of a backpack—that was hardly a recommendation, and yet there was something about him, something endearing. Maybe it's that he never stopped searching for that indefinable thing we all seem to be seeking, that something that we believe is out there but which always seems to be just beyond our grasp. Happiness. Was that what it was? Could you say something like that? Did you dare?

He would deny it if asked, but that was because his nature would not let him accept the possibility that you could have such a thing in this world. He had told her several times before that life and therefore happiness was negated by death. There is no security or stability, he liked to say. No one here gets out alive. There are no happy endings. But what if there were? What if they, she and Frank, could find it—together? Maybe a man and a woman could have such a thing. Maybe. She slid onto the couch next to him and put her arms around him. He stirred awake and smiled sleepily at her. She flattened down a cowlick in his hair with her palm.

"Sorry." He forced himself awake. "I tried to wait up for you."

She kissed him on the ear, the cheek, the mouth. He was awake and her light kiss became a shared one, long and loving. She pulled away when she felt his hands, insistent, begin to caress her body.

"Come on, honey." She stood, helped him up. "Let's go to bed."

———

THEY LAY ON TOP OF the covers in Kim's bed, she wore only his T-shirt, he only his undershorts. They spoke softly and clung to one another in post-love affection.

"Where were you going when you stopped by here?" She twisted Frank's graying chest hairs with her right index finger. He slid his left hand off her waist and rested it on the side of her hips.

"Biloxi, like I told you." He laughed lightly.

"What's so funny?"

"Oh, nothing. Just seems I get asked that question a lot. Nature of the trip, I suppose. Why did you want to know?"

"No real reason. It just seemed so coincidental."

"Well, I knew you had moved down here, but after we lost touch I figured you were long gone, the way you TV folk go from town to town and all."

"Were you hoping I was here?"

"I try never to get my hopes up, but I knew you were here once. It was a major lucky deal for me."

"Me, too." She kissed him softly on the mouth.

"You're a sweetheart." He hugged her.

"You know what I'm in the mood for?" She rolled toward him, letting her arm lie across his stomach.

"I don't think I'm ready again, yet."

"Not that, silly." She swatted his hand off her upper thigh.

"Then I got lucky."

"No, seriously, I'd like to have a cigarette."

"I thought having a smoke after sex went out with the Surgeon General's first nasty warning on the cigarette packages."

"It was just an urge."

He hopped out of bed and hustled into the living room, returning with his backpack before she could figure out what he was up to. He tossed the bag down beside her and jumped back in bed. She made a face at the backpack.

"I don't know what you're doing with that thing, but it certainly goes with your Toyota, old and worn out."

"Like me." He poured some of the contents of the bag onto the bed.

She play-acted like the stuff might be nuclear waste. He produced the pack of Marlboros he'd been hauling around since El Centro.

"What in the world are you doing with those? I thought you quit smoking years ago."

"I did. I don't know why I have them. I bought them on impulse right after I took off from San Diego."

"Can I have one?"

"Sure, but I didn't know you smoked either, till now."

"I don't really. I just like one now and then. Sometimes with a beer. Besides, somebody's supposed to light one up now, aren't they? It's in all the movies."

"Here." He handed her the pack.

She took one, found a lighter in the top drawer of the nightstand on her side of the bed, and fired up. She inhaled and then blew smoke out in a blue cloud.

"I wish I could do that." She offered him the cigarette. "No, no, I only mean I wish I could be like you and have one every blue moon. With me, it's one and, bingo, I'm back to two packs a day."

"You still smoke pot, though, don't you?"

"Yeah, but that's different. I'm like you and cigarettes, one or two rarely. But I think nicotine is a lot worse for you than weed any day—if you ask me, that is."

She stared at the cigarette, took another puff, and was searching for a place to put it out when the phone rang. Quickly delegating ashtray duties to him with a wink, she moved to an upright sitting position on the edge of the bed and answered the call.

Juggling the cigarette for a moment and nearly burning himself, he climbed out of bed and carried it to the bathroom to flush it down the toilet, recalling a time long ago when some friends had flushed a whole lid of grass against his objections in paranoid fear of a bust that did not occur. Grimly grinning to himself and hoping that the call didn't mean what he knew it meant, he walked back into the bedroom to find her getting dressed and already amazingly presentable.

"I'm sorry, Frankie." She saw his grim grin fade. "There's been a big chemical spill and fire down by the river front, and they couldn't get hold of Gina. I'm next on the list. I've got to go cover it. You're not mad are you?"

"No."

"Disappointed?"

"Yeah, you could say that."

"You know how this goes. I'm sorry. Better not wait up this time. It'll probably be early morning before I'm back."

"I should get myself together anyway."

She finished dressing and began collecting her reporter's gear. He helped her. When she had everything stowed into a deep, long-strapped cloth and leather day bag, she paused a moment as if to let his last words sink in. He could see the realization dawn in her intelligent eyes.

"You're not going to be here when I get back, are you? He couldn't answer right away. "Even after tonight?"

He strove for coherence. "I have to finish whatever it is that I'm doing now." From the moment the jangle of the phone had interrupted the night, he was sure he hadn't been thinking too clearly about anything. "That doesn't mean I won't be back."

"God, I hope it doesn't." She moved to him and hugged him tenderly. "It better not. Damn it."

"You're a beautiful woman, a beautiful person." He leaned forward and kissed her on the forehead.

"There's such a sense of fatalism about you, Frank."

"You have to know the rhythms of your own life."

"Walk me to the door." At the door, they paused and kissed. "We haven't said anything about love." She stared into his eyes.

"What would you think about getting a little place somewhere in the country and living together for a while?"

"You know how important my work is to me, Frank. Could you live with a reporter? This kind of thing like right now happens all the time."

"I know."

"It doesn't mean we couldn't have a life together, does it? You're not one of those men who can't live with a career woman. I know you're not."

"No."

He knew he could get past any residual hangups he might have about that. His fear was more visceral than that. He feared that this night was all the happiness that it would be his lot to have. He feared that whether he stayed or not, the happiness would be snatched from him regardless. At his core he deeply distrusted the reality of joy, happiness, as either might relate to his life.

"No." He repeated. "I'm not one of those guys."

"Then at least promise me you'll come back."

"Promise."

She hugged him again tightly, and they kissed once more.

"I've got to go, baby." She pulled away.

He reluctantly let her. Her eyes were moist, but she was not going to cry. He was within an inch of saying he loved her. He was at least that close to staying as well.

"I'll see you again." He told her as she started down the steps to her parking space below the condo.

"Keep a journal for me." She called back. "I want to know where you've been and where you end up going."

His voice wavered. "Okay."

He stood on the steps, watched her get into her car, start the engine, and turn on the lights. She waved up at him from behind the wheel, and he returned the wave. He remained outside until the tail lights of her car disappeared into the early Memphis morning. After a few moments, he slowly turned away from the quiet parking lot and went back inside, closing the door firmly behind.

23

FRANK SAT IN BACK OF the Harrison County courtroom in Gulfport while Stuart Malory worked the jury. Stuart was eloquent, well prepared, and confident without appearing to be arrogant. Frank could see why his ex's ex-brother-in-law had become one of the most successful trial lawyers on the Mississippi Gulf Coast. He also knew Stuart was terribly successful because his wife Cassie, who he had as yet never met in person, had informed him so when he'd called ahead to prepare them for his visit. After talking to Cassie, he expected the visit to be a short one.

Thinking of her and the unappealing image she projected over the phone served to drive his thoughts out of the present of the courtroom and into the recent past of Memphis. He let the image of a shrewish Cassie dissolve into the far more pleasant one of Kim.

He could still see her, fabulous in her blue jeans and work shirt, standing by the news counter at the New Mississippi when he had first driven into Memphis. And he pictured her muscular brown legs as she stood by the bear habitat at the Memphis zoo, wind blowing her hair back to reveal that fine, thin face in profile. And he remembered his last image of her down at the bottom of her townhouse steps walking away from him, proud and strong, to her car. And then the obvious, inevitable question. Why in the hell had he left her back there in Memphis? What was he thinking—or not thinking. He was an idiot, a fool. He knew it wouldn't be easy getting over her. If he ever did or even wanted to.

Maybe his trip had gone on far enough. Maybe it was time to call it off. To come in out of the cold. He imagined retracing his path to New Orleans and then heading right back up to Memphis where she would be waiting, he hoped, happy and affectionate, for his return. He breathed deeply and exhaled slowly, as if his longing could be purged from his system on the used up air no longer needed by his lungs.

He leaned his head back and closed his eyes. If he dozed, he did not realize it, but the next thing he knew, someone was shaking him by the shoulder. When he opened his eyes, the courtroom was clearing, and Stuart was at his side.

"How ya doin', Sport?" A smile widened across the barrister's clean shaven, heavy jawed face as Frank readjusted to his latest new environment. "What do you think of old Stu's courtside manner?"

"Hey, Stuart." They shook hands. "Sorry, I must have drifted off or something. Did you win your case?"

"Jury won't decide until tomorrow, but it's dollars to donuts we got it in the bag. Stuie Malory don't cut these Mississippians any slack. I'm the best in the biz."

"I knew that."

"Frankmeister, you old coot. Still got that sharp wit. I like it. Show's you're bright. You should've been a lawyer."

"I don't think so."

"Sure. You'd be terrific. Frank Mason, Attorney at Law. Got the last name for it, baby. Gotta be a winner. Grandson of old Perry. You'd be a star, instant hit."

"Uh-huh."

"Well, what'dya say?" Stuart's enthusiasm made Frank feel exhausted by comparison. "Shall we take a ride back up the coast a ways. Momma'll be waiting dinner for us, I suspect, by the time we get home."

"Sure." He stood. "That'll be fine."

Stuart patted him on the shoulder. "Let's get going. Let me tell you, I'm one hungry ambulance chaser."

———

THE DRIVE BACK UP HIGHWAY 90 to Biloxi gave Frank another chance to see what had happened to the area since he had been stationed there thirty years before. The most obvious change was how the place had built up. Years before it had been just another small southern town on the Gulf Coast, surviving principally because of Keesler Air Force Base, the shrimping industry, and by its proximity to New Orleans.

Now it was the Gold Coast with massive floating gambling casinos and huge resort hotels drawing the new yuppified southern middle class. He was duly impressed by the new glitter and glitz, but still felt the rhythms of the old south moving underneath it all. He said as much, but Stuart was quick to correct that impression.

"Oh, no, the only thing like that you'll find today would be strictly for historical reference, such as Jefferson Davis' home. This is the new South. We're entirely different."

"Every other part of the new south I've been in has just been the old one with a face lift."

"Lord have mercy, don't let Cassie hear you saying something like that now. Gracious me, she'd have a cow. She's extremely proud of being part of the new order down here."

"New order. What a load. All the new orders everywhere, new names, new buildings, new this, new that. Underneath—same old bull."

"Reserve a little judgement, Frank."

Stuart guided his little white BMW 325i convertible down the road past the Mississippi Coast Coliseum and Convention Center and on by the new hotels and businesses to the easterly edge of Biloxi—Frank looked vainly for recognizable landmarks from his days there—and then turned north, stopping to let him get the Toyota from the parking lot beside Stuart's law office.

With Stuart in the lead and Frank chugging along behind, they made their way through town to an upscale neighborhood bordering a golf course. Stuart motioned for him to park in the circular drive that fronted the house and pulled the 325i into a cavernous three car garage.

Stuart's home, he observed over the top of his hopelessly out of place car, was a virtual replica—though on a smaller scale—of an antebellum southern aristocrat's home, complete with white columns and wide-railed porch. It was a well-kept house, Stuart stressed as they strode up onto the front porch, a tribute to Cassie's considerable homemaking skills. Skills Frank noted were augmented by a groundskeeper for the vast willow-filled yard and numerous flower beds outside and by a housekeeper who worked in the expensive, shiny interior. Both workers were black and they carefully scrutinized Frank as he passed the man working in the front yard and then encountered the woman who grimly received them at the front door.

Stuart gave his briefcase and suit jacket to Evelyn, the housekeeper, and they went into the large family room to have a pre-meal drink. Frank leaned against the counter of the wet bar and pondered the utility of a large, brick fireplace across the room. It did get cool during the winter in Biloxi, but he couldn't imagine the feature getting much use.

Just as he was about to formulate an inane question on the topic, a tall, slender woman with thick, auburn hair came into the room. Stuart stopped mixing his gin and tonic and hurried over to greet her.

"Cassie, sweetheart." He gushed. "You're lovely. As always."

"Thank you, darlin." She offered him a well rouged cheek to kiss, which he did.

"Angel," Stuart put his arm lightly around her shoulder. "This is Frank Mason. Frank, Cassie."

"Nice to meet you." Frank used his most polite manner.

She turned her sharp green eyes on him, and he saw just the tiniest furrow in her brow for just the tiniest of seconds. As quickly as the furrow disappeared, a smile formed on her lips. One that was practiced, and, he surmised, that had often been used for dealing with people she didn't know and probably didn't want to. It took an effort on her part to produce it, and he found himself appreciating that effort despite his knee jerk reaction to her too prim and proper appearance and to her too thin lips and hawkish nose. This was a woman who had known what she wanted a long time ago and had been willing to pay whatever price it took to attain and keep it.

"Welcome to our home. Thank you so much for dropping by to see us on your way through town. Stuart has told me a lot about you."

"Thank you, Cassie." He felt his speech slipping back into old, comfortable patterns. "I appreciate it a lot. I just wanted to stop by and say hi before heading on east. I didn't intend to inflict myself on you all more than that."

"Nonsense, Frank, we're happy to have you here—aren't we, Cassie, dear?"

"Of course we are, sweetheart. Frank is most welcome."

"You gotta stay a couple of days at least. Tomorrow we're going out to Ship Island, and Sunday we'll hit the links right back here at the country club."

"That's really good of you, Stuart, but I only intended to visit for a bit and be on my way."

"Here." Stuart went back to the bar, leaving Frank and Cassie uncomfortably together. "Have a drink, rest a spell, and eat supper with us. We are still hospitable in this neck of the woods. What'll it be?"

"Beer. A light one if you have it."

"Well." Cassie announced. "I'd best see to supper, then. I expect you like seafood, Frank? We have the best in the world here, you know."

"Uh. . . ."

Stuart rescued him. "Just have Evelyn cook up a plate of fresh vegetables, honey." He carried in a large gin and tonic for himself and brought Frank a beer. "He's not a meat eater."

"Why seafood ain't meat, silly. It's shrimp and fish and such."

"Thanks anyway, Cassie." Frank apologized. "I'm sorry to put you out. A plate of vegetables would be fine."

"Heavens." She clucked. "What a peculiar world we have these days."

"I couldn't agree with you more, Cassie. I couldn't agree with you more."

"In any event, supper will be ready in a half hour or forty-five minutes. You men folk don't drink too much, understand?"

"Yes, er, no, ma'am."

"We won't, darlin'."

"I had no intention of staying and putting you all out." Frank turned to Stuart when Cassie had exited the room.

"Not a problem."

"What about Cassie? She must think I'm some kind of major weirdo sleaze bag."

Stuart chuckled. "Cassie can adapt to anyone—even you."

"I don't doubt it." He raised his beer to Stuart's glass in toast. "I don't doubt that one bit."

———

"I UNDERSTAND YOU'RE ON SOME sort of adventure." Cassie leaned back as Evelyn cleared away the dinner dishes. Stuart pushed his chair back to puff on a fat stogie and sip alcohol.

"I don't know if I'd call it an adventure. It's just kind of a long trip."

"Are you going somewhere special?"

"Hell." Stuart blurted out from somewhere his fourth gin and tonic had taken him. "He's out to discover America—ain't that right, Frankie boy? In quest of the holy American Grail."

"I don't know about that. I'm just driving across country. I don't know what I'm looking for."

"Sex, drugs, and rock and roll." Cassie rolled her eyes. "In search of lost youth, of hope, of love, of a final lay. That's it, isn't it?"

"Stuart, what must Frank think?"

"Shit—uh, shoot—momma, he's old family. We always go on like this."

"Not at my dinner table, please."

"I'm going to try and visit an old service buddy up in North Carolina." Frank returned to the topic. "And then go on to the coast. After that, I don't know."

"At least someone here still has some semblance of manners about him."

"It's his upbringing." Stuart burped. "He's a southern boy, you know."

"Is that right?" The honey in Cassie's voice filled the air between them.

"Yes, ma'am." Frank slipped into Southern mode almost against his will. "I was raised in Arkansas. But I left there a long time ago."

"You haven't been back since then?"

"A couple of times."

Stuart called to Evelyn for another drink.

"And I was stationed in North Carolina and here in Biloxi. That was quite some time ago, too."

"Well, I expect you'll find it quite different now. We've come a long way down here, progressive, modern—we like to think of ourselves as the New South."

"So I've heard." Frank stared directly into Evelyn's unfriendly eyes as she came up beside Stuart with his drink. "But except for the new roads and buildings, it seems much like the old south to me."

Evelyn gave Frank a withering look. Stuart took the latest gin and tonic and sipped on it contemplatively. Cassie felt compelled to defend the new southern order.

"Mercy, no. Why, not at all, Frank. Just in my lifetime we've seen the end of unfair living conditions and segregation and racial prejudice in general."

"All that happened right here in Biloxi?" Frank winked at Evelyn.

She raised both eyebrows, made a little puffing noise, and left the room. Stuart languidly watched her go. Frank reengaged Cassie.

"I don't mean to be combative, Cassie, but the only difference I see is that a new facade has been erected over an old structure. Sure, the 'colored only' signs are gone, there's some low income housing, and everybody's got food stamps, but by and large the races still live apart, play apart, work apart. Considering all the lip service paid to it, I don't think we've come too far."

"Perhaps Arkansas' not the same as Mississippi or perhaps you're only seeing the bad things any place has."

"Maybe and maybe I've not been to—"

Stuart slapped the palm of his hand on the table. "West Ship Island. Fort Massachusetts. That's what we'll do in the morning. You'll love it. Sunday we golf."

"Golf?"

"Golf." Stuart set his drink down.

"I should be taking off tonight." Frank glanced at Cassie. "Let alone staying two days more. Thanks anyway."

"No way, you're our guest. We'll boat over to Fort Mass tomorrow, and the day after it's golf. Hell, the course is right next door. We can walk to it."

"Honey, Frank said he had to continue on. I'm sure he has some other place he'd rather be."

"Yeah, I should go on."

"Nonsense. I haven't seen you in years. You can hang out for the weekend and then go on running around the country. What's the problem? Don't you like our hospitality?"

"Oh, no, it's not that. I just wouldn't want to impose on you, that's all."

"You're not imposing at all. Is he, Cassie?"

"No, of course not."

"Thank you, Cassie." Frank tried to emote his apologies through his eyes and expression. She turned away.

"All right. It's all settled, and that's that."

"Okay. So what's this Fort Massachusetts? I don't remember that from when I was stationed down here."

"Come with me." Stuart rose and motioned for him to do the same. "I'll tell you all about it."

He followed out into the den where he took a seat, uncomfortably, on the edge of a large easy chair while Stuart made a cozy little nest for himself on the end of a huge couch just to his right. While Stuart talked about the Ship Islands and the forts out in the Gulf, Frank looked through the door leading to the dining area. At the back of that room, Cassie and Evelyn were engaged in a vigorous conversation. From that distance, without the sound, it was hard to tell who was the mistress of the house and who was the maid.

24

BILOXI, MISSISSIPPI—1964

ILOXI, MISSISSIPPI AT THE END of August was hot, humid, and uncomfortable. For the three weeks before his technical school at Keesler Air Force Base was to begin, Frank alternated weeks of grounds-keeping duty and KP. Trips off base were at a minimum and limited to a dry cleaner and tailor shop, pool hall, and fast food restaurant just out the back gate.

For another five and a half weeks after that his free time outside class was taken up by advanced basic training. Off base jaunts were again limited and brief. But in mid-October the advanced basic ended, and except for occasional special duty he found himself with most of each afternoon off and, at last, a free Saturday with a day pass to go into town.

He and his new buddy, New Yorker John Carswell, hopped the ten o'clock shuttle in front of the base exchange and rode it to the city bus station. With hardly a glance at the grungy little terminal, they took out for downtown. Their first stop was a record store.

"Check out this Beach Boys album." Frank held it for Carswell to see.

"So what?" California beach music had failed to impress the mostly blue collar Irish neighborhood he came from in high upper Manhattan.

Frank slipped the record back in its place and searched for something else.

He thumbed past a couple of Beatles albums and a Dion and the Belmonts greatest hits collection. Then he found a Bob Dylan record.

"Hey, Cars, Bob Dylan!"

"Never heard of him."

"This is New York City on the cover."

"So, I don't know everybody in the whole damn city."

"I'm going to come back and get this on payday."

"Your money."

Frank replaced the Dylan record and walked around to the next aisle. Carswell came over, too. Frank found a Rolling Stones album and showed it to his buddy.

"Now you're cookin'."

"Payday."

They rummaged around for a few minutes more, then Carswell suggested they walk out to the highway and up to the USO Club.

"Let me ask the clerk something first." Frank went up to the counter. "Excuse me, could you help me?"

"Yeah."

"Do you know if you have a record by a group called the Rivingtons? It's got a song on it, I think it's called "The Bird's the Word."

"Never heard of it." The clerk seemed distracted or disinterested.

"Can you check?"

"Don't have it."

"The Rivingtons. The Bird's the Word."

"I said we don't got it." The clerk scrutinized him. "We don't carry it."

"Jeez."

"Asshole." Carswell said when they were outside. "What a butthole."

"Jeez."

"Friendly town, huh?"

The USO Club was in a big white Victorian house across the highway from some kind of factory-like buildings that hid the beach. They showed their IDs to a matron lady who greeted all the arriving GIs and then they walked over to a table with a punch bowl and several plates of cookies on it. Carswell gobbled up a handful and downed a cup of punch. Frank just stood around.

The lady came over to them when she saw them just hanging out by the refreshments. "The dance is upstairs."

"Thank you, ma'am." They went up to the dance floor.

From there you could see the grounds of the club—freshly trimmed grass, washed off sidewalks, cool shade from a big magnolia tree and a huge, cascading weeping willow.

They stood to one side and checked out the dancers. The girls were dressed in light colored, semi-formal, southern Gone-with-the-Wind dresses. Each had a number pinned to her left shoulder.

"Man, check that girl over there." Carswell nudged Frank and whistled.

He looked where Carswell nodded, trying not to be too obvious about it. "Jesus."

The girl was dressed like all the other girls. She had shoes like all the other girls. She was young and slender like most of them, but she didn't have any arms—or, rather, she had arms and hands, but they were just little stubs coming out of her shoulders. When she walked and danced, they swayed like she didn't have full control of them.

"Man." Carswell shook his head in admiration. "That girl's got pluck. She's really brave."

"I guess so." The sight of the girl made Frank uncomfortable, a little sad.

He couldn't help but think that she was probably being taken advantage of by the GIs—that is, if they were like most of the guys in his outfit, which he figured they were. He sipped his punch and concentrated on looking outside. After the shock of the girl began to subside, he realized his main feeling was one of boredom.

He told Carswell so.

"Let's make like a tree and leaf." Carswell tried to be funny. Frank wasn't in a funny mood.

"Come on."

They dropped their half full cups of punch in a trash can and, with parting glances at the short-armed girl, left.

Outside, Frank felt some better, and as they walked along the sidewalk on the north side of Highway 90, he soon forgot about the USO and the girl, though he was left with a nagging sense of discomfort, as though something was wrong but he couldn't exactly identify what. A couple of blocks down the road, they turned up a street heading up town and passed a small betting parlor.

They poked their heads in the front door. "I thought it was against the law to gamble." He looked at Carswell.

There was all kinds of betting information in the little parlor. Blackboards hung along the walls gave the early line on the weekend college football games and displayed the odds on upcoming prize fights and the winding down baseball pennant races. High on the wall behind a counter at the back of the room were more blackboards presenting racing lineups from around the country. The horse racing charts reminded Frank, though in a much less grandiose way, of the huge ones he'd seen in a betting house in Mexicali, old Mexico.

"They had the races from Santa Anita in there." He let Carswell drag him outside and up the sidewalk.

"Who cares? Let's get a burger. There's a restaurant up there."

"I thought it was against the law to gamble down here."

"God, you are a hayseed. California didn't teach you much, did it?"

"I don't know."

"Come on."

The glass-enclosed anteroom to the restaurant offered a cool respite from the humid, hot day outside, and they took deep breaths of the refrigerated air.

"I'm gettin' hungry as hell." Carswell pushed open the double doors into the restaurant proper.

"I could go for some fries, too."

Just inside, Carswell stopped in his tracks. Frank practically crashed into him from behind.

"What the—"

Carswell stood rigid, his left arm raised with his hand and index finger extended as if to quiet him or to point something out.

Frank peeked past to the waitresses who had paused in their work and stood staring at the two young GIs. He didn't know what was going on, but something was wrong. The place had gone stone dead silent, and no one moved. He noted the patrons who filled the place. They were all silent, halted in mid-bite or mid-drink, gawking at them, some hostile, as if they had just arrived in the restaurant from some alien land.

"What the hell?"

"Let's split."

Frank had never seen the brash New Yorker uncomfortable about any-thing before.

"I don't get it."

"Just back out of here." Carswell bowed grandly to the customers and wait-resses. "Go."

Frank turned, not comprehending, and hurried back out to the sidewalk. He felt a rush of steamy, sticky air and tugged at his sweaty shirt. Carswell quickly joined him, and they headed back up the street toward downtown. Back at the restaurant the waitresses busily tended to the customers who had returned to their meals as if nothing had ever happened.

"Cars, what the hell was that all about?"

"Southern hospitality, pal. Southern hospitality."

"C'mon, man, really."

"Well, hell, wasn't it obvious? GIs ain't welcome in that joint. I'd heard of stuff like that about down here before, but I would never have believed it if I hadn't seen it."

"I guess we have now."

Carswell nudged him. "Check it out. Now we're gettin' warm."

Up ahead to their left was a rundown old theatre.

"We can go in there if you're in the mood for a little chokin' of the old chicken." Carswell joked.

"Chokin' the what?" Frank gawked at the still displays showing women in various stages of undress and in postures considered by someone, perhaps a struggling chiropractor, to be provocative.

"Chokin' the chicken, you dumb Okie."

"Arkie."

"Excuse me, Arkie—Okie, whatever. Choke your chicken, flog your dog, whip your weenie, pound your pud, whack off, beat off, get it?"

"Got it."

"C'mon, you damn hillbilly." Carswell pried him away from the theatre displays. "Let's get a quick beer and head back to base. This place sucks."

"Cars." He waited until they had turned left back down the main drag and stopped in at the first of several wide open bars in the middle of the "dry" city to ask. "I don't get it. How come there are bars everywhere when it's dry down here? That cop out front didn't even check ut out when we came in."

Carswell swallowed the last of a pickled egg, took a big drink of beer, burped, ordered a pickled sausage from a big jar in front of them on the bar, and gave him the 'you-Okies-sure-ain't-been-anywhere' look.

"Money." He burped again after a bite of the sausage and rubbed the fingers of his right hand together. "Moolah, dough. That's all that counts. They don't give a damn about whether it's bad or not. It's all about making money."

"Jeez." Frank was impressed anew with his new friend's worldliness.

At the bus station waiting to go back to base, Carswell tapped him on the arm and pointed to the "colored" bathroom and waiting area signs.

"Can you believe these crackers?"

"They didn't have nothin' like this up where I'm from." The ticket clerk and a couple of middle-aged farmer types regarded them.

"A hundred years behind the times."

The base bus pulled into the station.

"You'd think they'd want to be part of the United States."

"Why don't you boys go on back to wherever it is y'all come from." One of the farmer types offered in a cold drawl.

"Maybe I will." Carswell sneered.

"C'mon, Cars." Frank steered him toward the door of the waiting bus. "Let's go back to base."

"Good riddance to bad rubbish." The ticket clerk called after them.

Carswell tried to turn back, but Frank pushed him on board. They settled into their seats near the driver.

"What a fucked up place. Nothin' but a bunch of dumbass crackers."

"They're not crackers. Crackers are from Georgia. These are just plain old southerners."

"Call 'em what you want, Frank. Seem much the same to me."

He supposed that was right, but didn't say it out loud. It was definitely a different kind of place with a different kind of people than what he was used to.

They didn't say anything else after that, just stared out the window at the passing town. The bus bumped and ground its smoky way back to the diverse enclave that was their base. For a place they had both professed to hate, base didn't seem quite so lousy after all, at least at the moment. By comparison to some places, it wasn't so bad, not so bad at all.

25

STUART DROVE CASSIE'S LONG, LIGHT gray Mercedes 500SEL down to the Broadwater Beach Marina where a surgeon friend of theirs kept his forty-five foot motor yacht for private fishing and Gulf touring. When he was establishing himself as a leading defense attorney in the area he had won a malpractice suit for the doctor, and the doctor, ever grateful, made himself and his boat available to the Malorys on a regular basis.

It was a beautiful, warm, clear day with the tranquil Gulf spreading out before them like a huge off-blue-green calm lake. With the smell of salt water and the sound of sea birds in the air around him, Frank let his discomfort with being in expensive luxury cars and on private yachts recede with each mile the big cruiser put between it and the Mississippi coast.

The doctor, an amiable, robust man with a weathered, reddish face, quickly bypassed Frank's disposition not to like someone of such obvious wealth. He particularly liked the way the doctor had knocked down the barriers of formality by insisting on being called Reed instead of Dr. Jacobs. Reed did not seem ostentatious about his money and impressed Frank by appearing to enjoy sharing his good fortune, at least in regard to the boat, with others.

Cassie and Reed's wife Hannah sat in deck chairs sipping gin and tonics, while the men gathered around Reed at the helm. Stuart gulped Bloody Marys and tried, unnecessarily, to impress upon Reed that, despite his obviously not rich appearance and quirky personality traits, Frank was really an okay guy. Reed steered the conversation toward other topics as easily as he maneuvered the yacht through the lightly rolling Gulf waters leading out to historic Fort Massachusetts on West Ship Island.

"So, Frank." Reed asked, when Stuart went below for a refill. "I understand you spent some time here on the Gulf coast before. Is that right?"

"I guess you could say that. I was stationed out here a long time ago."

"A Keesler boy, huh?"

"Yes, that's right."

"Gonna be in town long?"

"No, just passing through. Stopped to see Stuart. And Cassie."

"You go back a ways?"

"Uh, this is the first time I ever met Cassie. Stuart is the ex of my ex's sister. Whatever that means."

"She's not a bad woman, Cassie." Reed pointed down to the deck where the two women were casually chatting. "Once you get to know her."

"I'm sure." Frank waved at the women who had turned at that moment to look up at the helm. Sharp ears or down wind, he thought.

"And Stu, you know, saved my butt several years ago."

"Yes, I heard."

"Saved whose butt?" Stuart stumbled back topside with a fresh Bloody Mary in each hand. "Whose butt?"

"Mine and you better take it easy, or you won't even be able to see the Fort by the time we get there."

"I'll be fine." Stuart leaned heavily against the interior railing behind Frank.

"Do you know the Ship Islands out here, Frank?" Reed adroitly steered past a large fishing boat that crossed their path a little closer than might be expected.

"No, to tell you the truth, I never even knew they were here until today. I guess I wasn't adventurous back in my tech school days."

"Not much chance to be on a military base, I wouldn't imagine."

"No."

"Well, I think you'll find the islands interesting, quite a history they have. The whole region in fact."

"Are you a history buff, Reed?"

"Local history, southern history, yes."

"Knows it better than the locals." Stuart continued knocking back the Bloody Marys but seemed to be keeping most of his wits about him. "Frank's a southern boy himself."

"Is that right?"

"I was raised in the south, but I left a long time ago."

"Well, welcome back to the 'new' south."

"Uh, thank you." Frank shuffled his feet. "Glad to be back."

———

AFTER TOURING FORT MASSACHUSETTS, THEY went around the southern side of the island to a relatively unpopulated beach area where they went onshore for a peaceful picnic lunch and some refreshing drinks. Toward late afternoon, they settled comfortably into beach chairs beneath a small, but adequate canvas canopy Reed carried on board the yacht for such occasions.

With a few drinks in him, Frank began to relax—more so than he'd felt in a while. It occurred to him that it was a little off his usual path to be fraternizing with such a group of wealthy people, but he didn't much care at the moment. He'd achieved a stand off of sorts with Cassie. Reed's wife had been friendly enough while essentially ignoring him, and Reed himself seemed to be a genuinely decent man.

He had been well off for a long time and had no need to climb any more social ladders. Congenial was a fair description of him—simpatico, as someone might have said pretentiously a decade or so before. As for Stuart, who had kept drinking but hadn't gotten any drunker, he was just a successful middle aged man with a dominating wife and some influential friends. He and Frank went back a long way.

Sipping on a cool beer, Frank had to admit he was enjoying being outside, on the Gulf, feeling the warm moist air on his face, the crying of sea birds, the glassy reflections off the water—grateful for the hospitality he'd been shown.

"Reed, Hannah, everyone." He lifted his bottle. "A toast to your kindness in inviting me. I really appreciate it."

"Our pleasure, it's little enough to do for a guest."

Frank glanced at Hannah. "I learned some time back that nobody has to do anything for anyone else. So when someone does something for me, I try to remember to be thankful."

"You seem like a mild mannered person, Frank." Hannah looked him straight in the eye. "And yet Stuart here jokes so much about your political persuasion."

"Moi!" Stuart cried out, feigning hurt.

Cassie kicked sand at him, and in dodging it he had to struggle not to spill his drink. When he had regained his balance, he stuck his tongue out at her. She ignored him.

"Were you a sixties activist or is he just being silly as usual?" Stuart raised a hand to object, but a look from Cassie stopped him in mid motion.

"Not one of any consequence." In the softening light, Frank could see that in her youth, she had been an attractive woman. In truth, she still was. "I'm just one of the groundlings, a commoner."

"That's refreshing to hear. I don't suppose everyone could have been a radical in those days. As long as you're not one of those who's been on the, how do they say, lam for all these years."

"I'm on the lam all right." A brief flash of the Arizona AYUDA run crossing his mind. "But not from the law."

"Listen, Hannah." Stuart interjected. "Don't believe this guy. He's an unregenerate revolutionary wanna be. He's left of Leon Trotsky for Christ sakes."

"Leon who?" Cassie asked.

"Stu's just kidding around."

"Tell us about what you're on the lam for." Hannah took a sip from her drink. "If it wouldn't be too personal."

"Oh, it's not too personal, but it might bore you to tears."

"I know this story." Stuart stood and reached his hand out for Cassie. "C'mon, hon, let's go for a walk and let Frankie regale the Jacobs with his Kerouacesque tale of cross country adventures."

Frank chuckled. "I'll give them the short version, Stu."

"We'll be back in just a few." Cassie told the others.

"Not too long." Reed reminded her. "We should be heading back soon."

"Okay."

Hannah sat the drank down and clasped her hands together. "So tell us, how did this journey begin?"

Reed handed Frank a fresh beer and opened one for himself.

"I was in San Diego, and I had recently gotten divorced from Stuart's ex-wife's sister."

"Sounds complicated."

"Sort of, maybe, but you'll see as I go along, it's a common story."

26

HOW DO YOU LIKE THE BOAT, Frank?" Reed piloted them back to the coast with the lowering sun occasionally blocked out by thick, dark clouds.

"It's really powerful. Pretty, too. I've never been on anything like this before."

"Well, now you have."

"Have what?" Stuart stumbled up the stairs in mid-conversation, though this time without a fresh set of drinks.

"Frank was just saying he'd never been on a craft like this before. I believe the old gal has impressed him."

"Mustn't buy too much into Frankie's 'aw shucks' attitude, Reed. He's been around a bit more than he lets on."

"So I gathered."

"Cut me some slack, Stu. I really haven't ever been on a boat like this. And I was just admiring it. Though to tell you the truth, I do wonder what a rig like this would cost. If you don't mind me asking, Reed?"

"Let me just say, it cost a lot. A fair amount."

Stuart guffawed. "At least half a dozen bypass surgeries, eh, Reed."

"I don't do heart surgery."

"What kind of surgeon are you?"

"I'm an orthopedic surgeon—joint reconstruction, hip replacements, some sports medicine work."

"Really, is there a lot of that around here?"

"Which?"

"Hip replacements. Sports stuff. Both, I guess. Do you do arthroscopic surgery, too?"

"There's more of both than you would probably imagine. And, yes, I do arthro fairly regularly."

"Lots of people into sports these days."

"Exactly."

"He's done a few of the New Orleans Saints, Frank." Stuart noted. "Big bucks there."

"I assisted on a couple of Saints players a couple of years back. Their team surgeon was an old colleague of mine."

"Cool. Who were the players? Any famous guys?"

"Big offensive linemen. Don't remember their names. These poor devils must average at least one operation a year. Their knees are like Frankenstein's head."

"I saw a show on TV, *Sixty Minutes* or something like that, I think it was. It showed Jim Otto was basically crippled from all those surgeries."

"Not surprising, Frank. Their knees take a fearful pounding."

"What were we talking about before we got onto that pleasant topic?"

"You started it." Stuart reminded him.

"The boat. We were talking about the boat."

"Oh, yeah, the boat. Well, it's a beauty. Totally out of my league, but a beauty, nonetheless."

"Want to take the helm?" Reed asked Frank.

"Take the helm?" Stuart cried out in mock fear. "Don't let him do that."

"And why not?"

"You weren't listening on the beach? He's liable to confiscate it in the name of the commies and steer us directly into the dock of the People's Navy. Oh, lord, Reed, it's like putting Lenin in charge of Fort Knox—not a smart idea!"

"Mercy." Reed exclaimed when Stuart was done. "I do believe we'll have to stop off somewhere on the way home and get our shoes cleaned after a pile like that."

"We'll need a water cannon for the job, I'm afraid." Frank joked.

"What are you boys doing up there." Hannah called from down on the deck. "Acting like fools?"

"No acting required," Cassie added.

"You gals pipe down. I'm trying to talk Frank into piloting us back in."

"I warned him." Stuart waved his arms about.

"Sounds like a excellent idea to us." The women agreed.

"Uh, I don't know. Maybe for a minute or so, with Reed right here beside me. I've never driven anything bigger than a fishing or water ski boat."

"You'll do fine." Reed moved over to let Frank in front of the wheel.

The women turned away from the helm and back to their own conversation. Frank took the helm and held it loosely at first, afraid he might suddenly veer them off in the wrong direction, then gripped it so he could feel the bumps of the boat across the water. When he relaxed, he held on firmly but comfortably, and as he made adjustments in their course, he was surprised at the amount of real play in the wheel. Much more than the little boats he'd driven years ago on the Salton Sea and the Lake of the Ozarks.

"That's the spirit." Reed patted his shoulder. "You're doing just fine. Keep us on a course a bit to the north and give it a little more throttle if you've a mind to."

"My main objective will be to stay out of everything else's way."

"Excellent philosophy." Stuart wagged a finger. "Works for me."

"Well, Captain." Reed checked after Frank had steered in silence for a few minutes. "Besides being an avid sea dog, are you a golf enthusiast as well?"

"Not exactly. I probably haven't played more than eighteen holes altogether in my life. That is if you don't count a little nine hole par three course I used to play some about twenty years ago."

"Well, that'll do. You can join our foursome at the club in the morning—right, Stu?"

"Oh, I don't know." Frank tried to back track on the path Reed was laying out.

"Sure he could. Marty said he couldn't make it tomorrow, anyway. Frank'll work right in."

"Now, guys, I appreciate it." Frank pictured himself in his faded jeans and pocket T-shirt among the country club elite. "But I don't think so."

"Then it's settled. Clubhouse at seven, tee off at seven-thirty. By the way, you might want to throttle back and angle a little to starboard. That shrimper's coming in fast."

"Oh, jeez, I didn't even notice him."

"Don't kill us just so you don't have to go golfing." Stuart kidded.

"Maybe you better take over again, Reed." Frank felt like an incompetent pirate at the helm of a particularly unresponsive, stolen clipper ship.

"On one condition." Reed moved up beside him.

"All right, I'll play. But I'm warning you, I'm god awful at it."

"Atta boy." Reed clapped him on the back. He gladly stepped aside and let the real captain take over the wheel. "Now you're talking."

Reed deftly bypassed the shrimper and guided them on toward the approaching shoreline and the safety of the marina. Frank marveled as they neared the shore that a day such as this one—one of private boats, fine wine and Brie cheese, and isolated beaches—should be such a commonplace for some people and such a unique, foreign one for someone like himself.

At a younger age, he probably would have railed against the inequity of it all. Now, with little sense of community left in him and most of his anger gone—both simply from the accumulation of years probably—he was just mildly surprised to find himself in such a position. He knew he wouldn't stay in such an environment, but at the same time he knew it hadn't hurt him any to have seen a little bit of it up close.

Maybe he just didn't care much anymore. Maybe what other people want of you and what they think of you is not really important—it loses most of its meaning over time. You were on your own in this world. A free agent. You made all your own decisions, your separate peaces. That was the price you paid for independence, both its reward and its punishment. It was a philosophy he was becoming used to acting out. It was one he thought he could live with.

27

THICK BLACK RAIN CLOUDS HAD been building up over the Gulf since early morning. Now, as Frank drove through Pensacola, the storm intensified with earlier sprinkles turning into heavy raindrops and then to a steady downpour. He drove into the night-like day with the lights on. Concentrating on the rain-pelted highway between squeaky flappings of the Toyota's barely effective windshield wipers, he'd hardly noticed the three mile Pensacola Bay Bridge. Shortly after he reached the other side, he saw a sign for Pensacola Beach and searched for a cheap motel to wait out the rain. A few miles on, he spotted a sign for a place by the beach and turned off the road where a large arrow pointed the way to the right.

The motel sat back from the road, its vacancy sign glowing through the storm. Pulling up in front of the office, he shut off the Toyota, slipped on his baseball cap, and hustled out into the rain. He only had to run ten feet from his car to the office, but by the time he had pulled the door shut behind him, he was dripping water from top to bottom. Nobody was behind the desk when he came in, but a sweet-faced, heavyset lady shortly made her way out of a sparsely populated cafe in an adjoining room to wait on him.

"Afternoon, sir." She set an order pad and pencil on the glass desk counter. "Can we help you?"

"Yes, ma'am, I believe you can. I could sure do with a room right now."

"Just one person?" The woman wore a name plate that read Vera.

"Yes." He tried not to drip too much on the worn carpet of the office.

A whiff of cheap, greasy food came to him from the adjacent cafe. Cheap and greasy or not, the smell made him hungry. He had hardly eaten all day.

"That'll be forty-five dollars plus tax."

"Can I pay with MasterCard?"

"Of course you can, hon."

"Something smells good in there." He nodded in the direction of the cafe.

"Got some fresh, homemade apple pie, and hot coffee just waiting for you, if you've a hankerin' for it." She revealed a couple of missing teeth with a big smile. "After you get settled, drop on back in if you care to. Charlie, that's my husband there—the little, skinny guy behind the counter—he'll fix you right up."

"Maybe I'll do just that. Which way is. . . number twenty-three?"

She pointed to the right. "Just around this corner, honey."

He peered out the window at the unrelenting rain.

"Third room down, you can park right in front of the door."

"Thanks."

"Come back for a bite to eat now. Helps you get by this rain."

"Maybe a little later."

———

WITH THE RAIN STILL HAMMERING down and evening coming on, he pulled on a hooded sweatshirt he found at the bottom of a suitcase, grabbed his small day bag and headed for the motel restaurant for supper. Vera and Charlie were behind the counter when he came in. They seemed bored and were probably fretting over the empty cafe. A result most likely of the seemingly unending, melancholy rain.

"Evening, folks." Frank took a counter stool near the couple. He laid the day bag on the stool to his left and picked up a menu.

"Evening, Mr. Mason."

"Evening, ma'am."

"Evening, sir." Charlie added. "This is real duck weather, ain't it?"

"It's raining like the dickens."

"The special tonight's jumbo fried shrimp and french fries. We didn't get it on the menu there, but there's plenty if you'd like."

"Thanks, ma'am, but probably not." It wasn't even vaguely worth the effort to waste these people's time and test their understanding with a hashing out of his eating habits.

"We got burgers, cheeseburgers, and the like if that might suit. Or maybe a steak. Got some steak."

"Well, you know." Frank lied a little bit. "Seein's how I'm not super hungry, what do you say I order a grilled cheese sandwich with fries. Would that be okay?"

"Of course it would, hon, whatever you want."

"Steak is good, though."

"I'm sure it is. I think I'll go with the grilled cheese."

"And fries."

"And fries."

"You want to get that for our guest, Charlie?"

"Be right up." He headed off down the counter toward the short order grill.

"May I get you something to drink?" Vera pointed to the soda fountain on her right. "A coke or a Sprite. We might still have a beer or two left, even. Hey, Charlie, any of that beer left yet? Mr. Mason might like one."

"Call me Frank. Mr. Mason's my dad."

"Frank might like one." Vera corrected herself with a wink.

"I just don't feel much like a Mr., especially with folks like you all. And a glass of orange juice will be just fine."

"Orange juice it is."

"Call me Charlie."

"Hey, Charlie."

"Hey, Frank. Where you from?"

"I been living out in California." He felt Vera's benevolent gaze as she put a glass of orange juice on the counter before him. "But I've lived in several other places, too. I'm originally a southern boy. How 'bout you guys?"

"We're from Michigan." Charlie sliced the grilled cheese neatly in two. He put it on a plate and then buried it with hot, oily french fries.

"Oh, Hemingway country."

"How's that?" Charlie set out an unopened bottle of catsup.

"Ernest Hemingway, the writer. He wrote a bunch of stories set in Michigan."

He cleared a space to pour catsup on the edge of his plate. He dipped a fry in some of the thick paste and chewed it slowly, savoring each hot bite.

"Hmm." Charlie scratched his head. "I believe we've heard of him, but we left there a long time ago. It's a big state."

"Do you miss it?" Frank let Hemingway rest in peace. "It's beautiful country up there, I'm sure."

"Have you been to Michigan?"

He wiped catsup off his mouth with a quickly messy napkin. "No, I haven't, but I want to go some day."

"It is beautiful." Vera affirmed. "But the winters are just awful."

"I can imagine."

"Charlie retired down here and with some family money I got we managed to use that and a loan to open this place up. It's not much, but it's our life."

"It's a fine place. You should be proud."

"We're happy here." Vera beamed.

"I retired over in Fort Walton Beach."

Frank dipped the corner of the second half of his sandwich in a new pile of catsup. "That the next town from here, Charlie?"

"Of any size. There's some beach places on the island here and then Navarre Beach, but Fort Walton's the next bigger place—before Panama City, that is."

"Why Fort Walton?" He took a drink of juice. "Were you working around there?"

"Charlie's Air Force, Air Force retired."

"Eglin Air Force Base."

"Is that right? I was in the Air Force. But just for four years. That's all I could do."

"I was in for thirty."

Frank whistled. "Now that's a long time. What did you retire as?"

"I only made it to Master Sergeant. I just sorta got stuck."

"Shoot." Frank finished the grilled cheese. "Master Sergeant's up there. E-7, not bad."

"Okay, I guess."

"You want anything else?"

He polished off the fries. "I think I'm okay for now."

It was like he'd known the gregarious couple for half his life instead of half an hour. They were like an aunt and uncle he'd somehow rediscovered.

"Are you headed any place in particular? I mean, if it's not bein' too nosy or something."

"I think I'm heading for the coast, through the Carolinas, Charlie. Maybe Myrtle Beach." He finished the fries and slid the plate out of his way.

"That sounds exciting." Vera put the plate behind the counter.

"There have been moments."

The door out by the motel desk banged open and a drenched couple stumbled in.

"Excuse me. I better go help these folks out." Vera trundled off to see to the newcomers.

"You ought to keep a diary or a log or something if you've been travelin' all this way from California."

"Well, you know what?" Frank picked up his day bag and set it on the counter. "I've got a notebook and a pencil in here somewhere. Maybe I'll do just that."

He tilted the bag to unzip it. The pack of Marlboros slid onto the counter along with the pencil and some toothpicks.

Charlie's eyes lit up. "Say, could I bum a couple of them smokes from you? The old woman don't like for me to smoke, so I have to sneak around, and I'm out right now."

"Sure, help yourself." Frank found the notebook and placed it on the counter by the bag. He took one of the toothpicks to clean his teeth, put the rest of them back, and handed over the Marlboros.

"You don't seem like a smoker to me." Charlie ferreted away three cigarettes into his shirt pocket. "Thanks."

"I'm not." Frank returned the pack into the bag. "I just been hauling these around since California. I don't have any idea why. Is that enough for you?"

"Plenty. I'll buy more later when I get the chance."

"Vera doesn't like for you to smoke, huh?"

"Naw, she don't. Says it's bad for me. But she don't really nag me, you understand. She's a decent woman. Just watchin' out for my health is all."

"I can see that."

"Are you married, Frank?"

"Was."

"Uh-huh." He felt the pocket of his shirt like he thought the cigarettes might be sticking out for Vera to see and disapprove of. "Kids?" When he had reassured himself his secret was safe.

"No, fortunately. Divorce is tough on kids."

Vera returned from the office. "What's tough on kids?"

She was such a classic, chunky, good-natured, lower middle class woman that she could have been emblematic of her entire social type. She and Charlie were what people used to call the salt of the earth. They were eminently likable.

"Frank was saying that he and his ex-wife didn't have any kids."

"That's too bad. I bet you'd have made a fine father."

"How about you all?" Frank skipped over Vera's evaluation of his fatherly potential. Over the years, lots of people had told him he would make a good father. They had all been wrong. "Do you have kids?"

"Yes." Charlie answered after a pause during which Vera briefly looked away from the men. Frank got a sinking feeling he'd asked the wrong thing.

"We had a girl and a boy." Frank thought he saw tears welling in Vera's eyes. "She went to the university."

"Over in Tallahassee."

"That's right. Tallahassee."

"Florida State."

"The Seminoles." Frank put in.

"Uh-huh." Charlie grunted approvingly.

"And she graduated?"

"Yes, now she lives down by Clearwater."

"New Port Richey." Charlie interjected, as if the name would make it all clearer to Frank. Frank wasn't even sure where Clearwater was, much less New Port Whatever.

"Right, she's an eco... ecole...."

"Ecologist?" Frank finished for her.

"That's it. That's a hard word to say. Anyway, that's what she does."

"Works for some firm helpin' clean up the Gulf."

"You must be really proud of her. That's a big-time thing to be nowadays."

"We sure are."

"Yer bet. It's all right as long as it ain't too much of a do-gooder thing and ruins business. Then it ain't so hot." Charlie was a realist.

"How about your boy?"

"The boy took after me some. He went into the service."

"Army, not the Air Force." Vera recited as if part of some age old litany.

"That's right. He was in the Army."

There was a long pause during which the tears welled up again in Vera's eyes. Charlie shuffled around behind the counter, not really doing anything.

"He was killed in Vietnam." Vera finally spoke softly.

Charlie added the explanation. "Our boy was one of the last ones sent over to that god-forsaken place. He was just eighteen and had only been there a few weeks when the place started to collapse. You seen those pictures of helicopters on top of the U.S. Embassy in Saigon?"

"Yes, I have."

"Our boy died in that Goddamned retreat."

"Now, Charlie."

"Pardon my French. That's how it happened."

"I'm sorry."

"It was a terrible war."

"Yes, it was."

Charlie shook his head. "Never could make heads or tails of it myself. Never made no sense to me. What did you think, Frank?"

"Oh, I heard a lot of reasons, but it never really made any sense to me, either."

"It just seemed to be about losing things. Especially after we lost our boy. Losing someone is the hardest thing of all, isn't it?"

"Yes, it is, Vera. Losing someone has to be the hardest thing of all."

28

FRANK SAT IN THE MOTEL room watching rain fall. It was no longer a torrential downpour but a steady, unrelenting rain. It made a pleasant drumming sound on the roof and poured out of the drainpipes onto the saturated ground without pause. Small streams of muddy water crisscrossed the grounds in seemingly haphazard, yet intricate patterns.

Pensive, he measured out another quarter glass of red wine from the bottle Vera and Charlie had somehow managed to find for him and took advantage of the lull in his travels to consider beginning the trip log he'd been thinking of starting and that both Kim and now Charlie had suggested.

If nothing else, it might help put what he was doing into some kind of perspective. He was practically to the east coast—the thought startled him a little—and hadn't even really considered what he was doing. Or where he'd been. Or where he might be going. Opening the log notebook, he wrote down a couple of headings and began listing people and places from the trip so far.

San Diego seemed so distant now that it was hard to believe he'd ever lived there. It was a lovely town in many ways, especially for California, but he'd never really felt a part of its essential life, its rhythms and personality. Of course, going through a divorce and working at a job he hated tended to produce feelings like that, anyway.

San Diego to El Centro, he jotted down, recapping his completed itinerary, the sand dunes in the Imperial Valley, Indio, Tucson, Boulder, mid-Missouri, then over to Columbia, down to Memphis, Biloxi, the Florida panhandle. An erratic enough pattern. Obviously the movements of somebody on the run. Heading in the same direction as Fonda and Hopper's rebels but more like a latter day, solo version of Kerouac or Kesey without the craziness. Or without most of the craziness. It had been a little crazy at times.

Now he was just drifting. Drifting toward the Carolinas and the coast. Drifting toward what? He didn't know the answer to that. If he had known, he'd have gone straight to where it was and skipped all the stops along the way. He was moving on instinct, searching for a geographical cure. But a cure for what? How do you cure yourself of being you? How do you change? What do you do?

Possibly his identity was tied up with women—or *a* woman. There had been wonderful women. Mattie, Terri, Kim.

Mattie, of course, was just an old friend. He loved her, but he didn't think of her as a potential partner, a mate. Terri had been a wonderful, unexpected gift from the powers that be, and that was all. But for what it had been, a brief interlude in a usually boring life, he was grateful.

As for Kim, his time with her had been almost too much to believe. Thinking of her and Memphis filled his mind with images that were hard to focus on, to remember clearly. Had she really come home that evening or early morning and had they made love? Did she actually care about him? Him, Frank Mason?

Disturbed by the welter of conflicting feelings and emotions Kim's image had triggered within him, he jumped up and paced the room. Love is secondary. It's what you do in life that's important. What counts is the mark you leave. But what if you don't leave a mark? What if you are just one of the many billions, the ignored, the forgotten, the never heard of? What then? What matters then?

If a person struggles to find their destiny, strives to reach that alignment of internal and external forces that is perhaps attained by so few—if a person tries and tries their whole life and finally realizes that outward destiny, the one that life had in store for them, was different from the destiny they dreamed of, thought was theirs, well? Well then, what?

To never find out what you were supposed to be or never to become what you believed, hoped you would be—what was the remedy for that? And, oh, how many times must that be and have been the case in the history of human-kind? Ninety-nine percent of the time, probably. Such a bitter thing. Not to become who or what you wanted to be. And that one percent. God, how fortunate, how incredibly lucky they were.

He stopped pacing before one of the front windows. The curtain was drawn back, the shades pulled up. The view of the drumming rain was unobstructed. It fell in a steady gray descent. He used to love going for walks in the rain. No one else usually went outside in the rain. You were safe. And alone.

Crossing back by the bed, he picked up a coat from the back of a chair and slipped it on. Kind old Charlie, loaning me his poor dead boy's raincoat. What sweet, lonely, lovely people. Pouring himself another quarter glass of wine, he tossed it down with one big swallow and headed for the door. A walk on the beach sounded like what he needed right then.

———

THE SURF WASN'T ROUGH, BUT the waves were big enough to push water across the soaked sand almost up to where he slogged along the beach in the rain. The mild roar of the waves was followed by the swishing of their white, bubbly residue running up the beach, putting him into a metaphysical mood.

You tried to stay on top of the waves of change and not get drowned by them. You tried to ride them as far as they would go, as far as they would let you, as far as you could. Maybe they were taking you to a better place. To a place that would be vital, dynamic, alive with human potential, of rea-son-tempered hope.

A place of freedom perhaps, where the value of the future and of the past would be of equal significance. A place that was fully alive and committed to making the best of the only time that really exists—the present. Because when all was said and done, it was only that split billionth of a nanosecond, that steady, moving stream of infinitesimally brief and unstoppable flashes of awareness that constitute this elusive thing called the present. That was all that mattered.

It was easy enough to say—live in the present. People have been saying it for millennia. But it was another thing to do it. Few people he ever knew—if any—really lived in the present. Most, including himself, lived in their thoughts, projecting the future, rehashing the past. But that was in our minds. In our real, physical life, most of us were living behind time. Trapped in some phase of our past like an insect in amber. We all became dinosaurs to one degree or another.

Popular music worked as an accurate, if unscientific, measure of this entrapment. Some people he knew had frozen in the 50s and early 60s so that anything from the Beatles on wasn't the same as before, wasn't as good. Some people never came out of the 60s—he remembered his own painful progress here. They remained flower children or hipsters or political activists, and they were still locked into the Stones, Hendrix, Joplin.

The 70s produced the wasteland of disco and wimp rock, then spawned the country outlaws, the punks, and the new wavers, all of them sliding into the cultural desert of the 80s. And of late? Rap, grunge. What was that about? Where did that generation—Generation X—where did they live? Maybe you lived in the present when you were young. Maybe. For a little while. After that it was jobs, families, freezing into place.

Or maybe that was all wrong, and the music metaphor didn't hold. Maybe it was an Eastern thing we Westerners were missing. Maybe it was all Maya, all illusion. We Occidentals were always moving, changing, chasing time. Maybe by moving out of time, by dropping out of it—like Duane and Mattie perhaps had done—maybe you could eventually move back into the stream of it and find your time, the time that was meant for you.

All his life, except for a brief five or six month period during 1970 when he was going to school in Missouri, he had been out of synch with time. Always a few years behind the big movements, the typical phases that people go through in their lives.

He was a little older than the majority of his generation that came of age in the 60s, so he had come to that era's mass movement late. He was late to go to college, to grow his hair, to demonstrate. And then afterward, late to enter the work force, late to marry. Always a step behind. Living a little out of step, living behind time. Was it a common malady?

Pausing along the shore for a moment, he realized he had been so absorbed in his inner ramblings he'd lost sight of the motel and that his shoes and raincoat were soaking wet. Turning around, he splashed back the way he came. The rain peppered the surf as it rolled up to his water logged shoes. He wasn't in a hurry to get back. The rain was heavy still, but it wasn't cold. He strolled along and let his thoughts go where he knew he'd wanted them to go all along. To Memphis. To Kim.

It seemed like a long time ago, but it had only been a few days. And if Memphis and Kim were long ago, San Diego and Laura were lost in the mists of prehistory. He had been a different man in Memphis from the one who had left San Diego. Who he was now was different from who he had been even in Memphis. He wasn't sure what had changed or was changing about himself, but he knew he felt like a different person.

As for the time he'd spent in Memphis, it was like a blur to him now. It had developed so fast, so much faster than he could have imagined, much faster than was usual for him. Relationships didn't happen that way in his life. Or they hadn't before.

Now he distrusted the memory, what he remembered happening. Did Kim really care about him? Did he care about her? One of the things he hated about himself, and suspected happened to everyone, was that with time and distance, even the most powerful feelings declined, diminished, faded away altogether.

That was fine for the painful experiences in life. It let you get past them, to go on. The trouble was that the same mechanism was at work on the positive experiences, too. And so what you were left with in the end was an accumulation of dulled memories, recollections without feelings, a sense of incompleteness and dissatisfaction.

Maybe Kim had just fallen in love with whom he used to be when she had known him out in San Diego. Maybe he only loved her because she was a weekend anchor person. Maybe those were okay reasons. He reached the motel and turned up from the beach toward his room. Maybe when you get to be a certain age, any reason for love was just as valid as any other.

Why not? He opened his door and stepped out of the lessening rain and into the pleasant dryness of the room. Why the hell not? Besides, he knew there were plenty of other reasons for caring about Kim. A woman sure as hell didn't have to be a high profile success story to be worth loving. It was who she was that counted, not what she was.

Yawning, he took off the raincoat and hung it up to dry. Then he undressed, draping his clothes on chairs, tables, anywhere to dry. He put on fresh under-clothes, comfortable dry socks, pulled on a pair of sweatpants and flopped on the bed, immediately tired. Yawning steadily, he clicked on the TV and lay back while some old sitcom replayed.

He was sound asleep before the first commercial break, his breath coming in a slow, relaxed pattern. He slept right through the rest of the afternoon, unaware of nightfall, sleeping the kind of sleep he used to when he was young, the kind he hadn't had in years. The kind he had never expected to have again.

29

THE MORNING DAWNED CLEAN AND fresh. There were scattered patches of light fog, but they were quickly absorbed back into the stunningly clear blue Gulf sky. Frank stood in the doorway of his motel room for about twenty minutes, breathing in the air as the fog slowly dissipated.

He had slept long and well and felt rejuvenated. Ready to continue on, but with a whole new attitude. The intensity of whatever it was driving him across the nation had diminished. He was calm, relaxed. Almost happy. He still wanted to finish the trip, but the sense of urgency about it had lifted, dissolved into the fresh Gulf air. He took a deep breath and exhaled loudly, thanked the powers that be for another day.

When the fog cleared, he prepared to leave. After a leisurely shower, he dressed and took his own sweet time packing what few things he had. Among them were the Marlboros, and he wondered at the peculiar impulse that made him buy them back in El Centro—was it a hundred years ago?

Taking the log book and a pencil out of the back pack, he sat at the room's little table and jotted down several memories and impressions from the trip. They were mostly memory fragments. How hot it was in the Imperial Valley, the highways he took through Missouri, the trees outside Jesse Hall in Columbia, the color of Kim's eyes, the length of the boat Reed owned in Biloxi. Details to help him remember the places, the events, the people. He found he was enjoying writing in the log and put down as many times, locales, and highlights as he could quickly recall.

When he was satisfied he'd taken a good set of notes—or at least enough for the time being—he closed the book and stored it and the pencil in the pack. He stood up, stretched and yawned contentedly, then set about organizing his few things to begin the trip again. He carried his bag out to the Toyota, then came back for the raincoat. He tossed it over his shoulder casually and walked slowly up to the restaurant to have a bite to eat and say goodbye to Vera and Charlie.

When he came into the office, they were at their usual posts, she behind the motel desk and he out working the restaurant, which had a half dozen or so patrons this morning—as busy as Frank had seen it.

"Good morning." Vera looked up when he approached the counter. "How are you this fine day?"

"Couldn't be better. I feel really fine this morning."

"All that darn rain finally got out of here."

"Yes, but it gave me time to think about things." He patted the raincoat smooth.

"That's good."

"Thank you all for loaning me this. I know it's special to you. I wore it when I took me a long walk yesterday."

"I know." She took the coat and laid it on a rack behind the counter. She also patted it smooth. "I could see you out there. Sometimes a little time alone in the rain does a body good."

"That's exactly right."

"Well, I'm hungry today. Think I'll go in and see what Charlie's got cookin' back there. A man needs a little food for the road."

"Are you leaving us, then?"

"I've got to go on."

"Of course you do. You go on in. Charlie'll fix you right up."

"I'll say my goodbyes before I leave."

"You better."

"See you in a little bit."

"All right."

Inside, he found an empty stool down the counter to the left of several other customers. Charlie nodded to him as he went by and, after putting several dishes out on the counter for the people who'd already ordered, he came on down.

"What'll it be, bub?"

"Well, sir, if it might be possible, I believe I'd like a stack of those silver dollar sized pancakes pictured so delightfully on your menu here. That is, if it wouldn't be troubling you too much."

"No trouble a'tall. We're proud to serve anyone here."

"Well, there's your problem, 'cause I sure wouldn't want to eat anywhere that would have me as a customer."

"That's a good one." Charlie slapped his apron-covered. "You're a card, son, a real character."

"How you doin' this mornin'?"

"Doin' fine. How 'bout you?"

"Better'n a long time. The rain seems to have washed something away."

"It'll do that."

"Thank you for the use of the raincoat. I appreciate it. I know what it means to you."

"I know you do. I could tell you would right away."

There was a pause and the two men looked away from each other. Neither knew how to fill that particular gap of silence, nor what would go into it. They were smart enough not to try.

"So it's little pancakes, eh?"

"Yes, sir. And a large orange juice, please."

"Be up in a jiffy." Charlie moved off toward the grill. "Want the juice now or with the meal?"

"With the meal. I'd rather wait."

The pancakes and a light covering of dark Karo syrup tasted wonderful. The juice cleaned out the excess sweet from his mouth, leaving him full and satisfied. He delayed finishing as long as he could, but finally pushed away from the counter and stood. Charlie was at the other end, waiting on a big trucker. Frank put a dollar tip under his empty juice glass and walked slowly out.

"Gotta go?" Charlie looked up as Frank came by.

"Gotta go, Mr. Charlie."

"Wait up there a little with Momma, would you? I want to say goodbye."

"See you up there."

"Well," Vera drawled, when Frank got to the outer check-in counter.

"Well." He handed her the check and a ten dollar bill.

She rang up the sale and gave him his change. As he pocketed the money, Charlie bustled in from the restaurant.

"Can't stay long, got a lot of customers this morning. But I wanted to wish you the best of luck, Frank. We've enjoyed meeting you."

"Same goes for me, folks. Me, too."

"Please come see us again sometime." Vera's eyes were moist again.

"I will, Vera. I promise."

"We're holding you to it, son."

"You do that, Charlie."

"Bye. now."

Vera came around from behind the desk and gave him a big hug. Charlie reached across the counter and they shook hands.

"So long."

"Goodbye, folks." Frank released Charlie's hand and gently disconnected himself from Vera's hug. "Thank you for everything."

He kissed Vera on the forehead above her tear-filled eyes and gave Charlie a thumbs up sign. Charlie returned it. Unable to say anything else, Frank turned and quickly left the office. He never let himself look back, though he felt the old couple's eyes on him all the way to the Toyota.

30

WAYNE PIKE'S TOBACCO FARM WAS between Raleigh and Wilson, some six miles off the main highway down a narrow blacktop road that reminded Frank of every redneck southern movie or story he'd ever seen or read. He could picture O'Connor's Misfit coming from the other direction to Shanghai and murder him. It was backwoods southern country, and though lushly beautiful, it stimulated in him a heightened sense of not belonging, of being an outsider.

"What a load." He rejected the impression decades of absurd Hollywood and Madison Avenue swill had managed to create. He figured *Deliverance* alone had set back the South's image by thirty years at least. "Christ, I was stationed out here for God's sake. Get serious."

Yet, when he spotted the mailbox reading *Pike* and pulled into the gravel driveway heading up to Wayne's double-wide, he couldn't entirely shake a residual sense of discomfort and nervousness. The dogs and kids that came running at his car didn't help matters much, either.

Through half-lowered glass, he considered the two hounds howling for his blood and the four little peckerwood kids pressing in front of the dogs to point and giggle at him. Despite his discomfort, he perceived the predicament as amusing. Maybe not as amusing to him as to the kids, but amusing nonetheless.

"Those your dogs?"

"No, they's the gover'ments.'" The oldest of three dirty-faced boys, a budding populist, declared. "Everything around here is, our daddy says." He and his siblings giggled.

"Well, is that right, Mr. Wise Guy?"

Frank figured the spokesman to be about twelve or thirteen, the girl about ten, the two younger boys maybe eight and five. Their large brown eyes, narrow noses, high foreheads, and thin mouths easily identified them as Wayne's progeny. The boys were all barefoot and wore dirty blue jeans and dirty T-shirts. The girl wore a clean but worn light blue summer dress and tennis shoes.

"So you guys going to call off the dog police so I can get out or what?"

"Or what, Mr. Stranger Wise Guy." The girl smirked and dramatically lifted her chin, snooty style.

The boys cracked up again. Frank was working on a retort in the salvo with the little group of country attack munchkins when he heard a door slam on the double wide. He looked up to see a thick-boned woman, presumably the kids' mom and Wayne's wife, standing in front of the trailer. She waved to him and signaled to the kids.

"Get those dogs outta there right now. That's liable to be Mr. Mason. Now get 'em away from there, and leave the man alone."

"Yes, momma." The girl drawled.

The boys, who were still giggling, helped corral the dogs and managed to shove and drag them a few feet away from the Toyota. The dogs stopped barking and Frank got out of the car. The woman hurried out to greet him.

"Mr. Mason?" She met him at the front of the Toyota.

"You must be Margaret, Wayne's wife."

"Why yes, I am." She offered him a work-toughened hand. His felt soft by contrast, soft like the white collar world he'd lived in for years.

"Yes, I am Frank Mason. And please call me Frank. Mr. Mason sounds like I'm my dad or something." The kids snickered until their mother gave them a stern look.

"Well, we're pleased to meet you. Children, this is Mr. Frank Mason. Mr. Mason, this is my oldest, Nathan. The girl is Melissa, and those two little ragamuffins are Wade and Bubba."

Frank winked at the kids. "Hello, Nathan, Melissa, Wade. And this one's Bubba, huh?"

"His real name's Harold Lee." Wade stuck his tongue out at his brother.

Bubba took a swing at Wade, who dodged it. Melissa stepped between the two, causing the dog Wade was holding to jump around and bark, which made the one Nathan held do the same. For a minute, it was like a pack of banshees had exploded out of some hidden hell hole.

"You children stop that this minute." Margaret commanded, disentangling a confusion of dogs and kids. "Nathan, you and Wade take Buck and Joe out back and put 'em behind the fence. For heaven's sakes, it's like a madhouse out here. What will Mr. Mason think?"

"Frank. Call me Frank."

The two older boys hauled the dogs off around the side of the house. Things settled down.

"Oh, my. Why are we standing out here? You must think I'm a terrible hostess. Come inside, please."

"Nothing of the sort." Frank followed them up to the house. "I think you're a really great family."

"That's kind of you. It can get a little wild as you've seen."

Inside the double wide he was surprised at the amount of room. Despite a general, lived-in clutteredness, the place was just fine. It had a smallish kitchen-dining area to the right as you came in, but the living room, which extended out from it, while not huge, was adequate. While Bubba raced down a hallway where Frank assumed the bedrooms and bathroom were, Melissa and Margaret scurried around the living room trying to tidy it up.

"I hope I haven't come at a bad time." Margaret stacked a pile of toys in one corner of the living room.

"Oh, no, no."

She went about straightening a sheet that covered a long narrow couch sitting in the middle of the room. The couch faced the back wall of the trailer and a big TV set. Done with her task, she looked up.

"Won't you please sit down?"

"Thank you."

"We got cable." Melissa said proudly.

"Cable's good."

"I believe these kids would watch TV all the live long day if we'd let 'em."

"Well, it tends to be that way with the young ones."

Bubba burst back into the living room and stationed himself directly in front of Frank. "Looky here, Mister." He held out two toy figures in his hands.

"Ninja Turtles." Frank carefully examined the pieces.

Bubba held up his left hand. "This here one's Donatello." Frank sized it up as if appraising a rare stone.

"And this one?"

"That's Rafael." The boy was serious, but Donatello had sounded like *Don O. Tello* and Rafael like *Rayfeel*.

"Well, you're a real Ninja Turtle fan, aren't you?" Frank acted like he was going to poke Bubba in the belly with his finger. Bubba grinned and stepped back.

"Oh, Bubba, Mr. Mason don't want to see your turtle things."

The boy seemed a little forlorn, so Frank tousled his hair. The boy walked over and plopped down on the opposite end of the couch. Frank winked at him. He hid his face in his hands.

"Would you care for something to drink, Mr. Mason? We got water and tea and some soda. Wayne's got beer in here, too, if you'd like one."

"Water would be fine, but please, call me Frank."

"Frank." Bubba said softly.

"That's right."

"Bubba!" His mother wagged a finger at the boy. "Melissa, please get Mr., uh, Frank some water."

"Thanks, honey." He took a drink, cold and refreshing, with more than a hint of mineral in it.

"I'm sorry Pike ain't here, but he's busy with the crop. I expect him directly. Nathan and Wade probably went to tell him you're here."

"Don't worry about it, Margaret. You got to make a living first. 'Sides, I didn't give you much chance to prepare for a visitor. But I couldn't pass up an opportunity like this to see Wayne."

"Heavens, we'd a been disappointed if you didn't come by. That's all Wayne talked about after you called."

"Good."

He took another long drink of water and leaned back on the couch. He would have preferred to sit in a chair facing the door so he could watch for Wayne but didn't want to seem ill at ease for fear of slighting Margaret. Fortunately the wait wasn't long.

Bubba was the first to signal his dad's arrival. He hopped off the couch. "Here comes Poppa's truck."

A wave by Margaret checked the little boy's inclination to race to the door. Frank couldn't hear the pickup till it was crunching gravel near the house. There was the sound of doors shutting, something metal banging together after that and then the front door opened. Frank set his glass of water on an end table and turned toward the door. With explosive energy, Nathan and Wade burst into the room, knocking Bubba over as they rushed in. Right after them came Wayne.

He spotted Frank. "Well, I'll be damned. Look what the cat drug in."

"Pike!" Margaret admonished her husband to the delight of the kids.

Bubba put his hands over his ears and rocked back and forth. Frank made his way from the couch over to shake hands with Wayne.

"You big old country ox, you." He pumped Wayne's broad, thick hand. "You ain't changed a bit, except you're bigger'n ever."

"And you still a wimpy little old ex-flyboy." Wayne pushed back the Caterpillar baseball hat he wore to reveal a head of shaggy but thinning hair.

"Hey." Frank pretended insult, sending the kids into peals of laughter. "I resemble that remark."

"I reckon you met my family?" Wayne handed a pair of dirty work gloves to Melissa, who took them and disappeared into the back of the trailer. She was back and standing beside Frank by the time he finished his answer.

"Yes, I have. We've been visiting while we were waiting on you."

"Darn if it ain't been a long time."

"A real long time."

"Well, boy." Wayne put his arm on Frank's shoulder. "You are a sight for sore eyes."

"You, too, old buddy."

Wayne turned to Margaret. "Momma, we gonna have us somethin' good tonight for supper?"

"Pizza!" The kids screamed out simultaneously.

"Not pizza when we have a guest." Margaret glanced at Frank.

"Actually, pizza sounds tasty to me, too. You don't have to go to any trouble, and on top of that, it's on me." The kids let out a cheer.

"I don't know." Margaret began doubtfully.

"Hey, boy." Wayne pointed at Frank. "It's your call. Some of us folks have to work for our money."

"That's probably true." Frank contemplated Wayne's dirty boots, jeans, and soiled shirt. "So what do you all say? Pizza on old Uncle Frank?"

"Pizza on old Uncle Frank." Melissa cried happily. Bubba echoed her a second behind.

"Oh, my, children, oh, my." Margaret leaned against Wayne. He put his arm around her and kissed her on the forehead.

"We're all a little too much for Momma sometimes."

She dug her elbow into Wayne's ribs. "Stop that, Pike. I just cain't imagine what Mr. Mason must think of us. A bunch of wild Indians, I suppose. And inhospitable ones, too."

"I think you're all great. Don't you worry about that stuff with me, Margaret."

Wayne whistled. "Who you think that boy is, the governor or something? That's old Frank Mason. My buddy. We go back a long ways."

"A long ways." Frank tapped his own thinning hair to the accompaniment of giggles from the kids.

Wayne rough-housed Margaret until she gave in.

"Pizza it is, then." The kids clapped their hands in joy.

"Git off me, you big lummox."

"Oh, watch it, Momma's on the warpath."

She gave him another dig to the ribs to the delight of the children.

"Well, listen, Frank. Want to take a quick tour of the farm before we eat?"

"No." The kids groaned.

"Sure."

"Don't be long. The young'uns is hungry."

"Just a little while." Wayne promised.

"Can we go, too, Poppa?" Nathan asked for the rest of the kids.

"Naw, I'm just goin' to show him the place real quick. Y'all stay here."

"We'll have fun at supper." Frank told the kids. "Pizza."

"Pizza!" They cheered.

"C'mon, boy." Wayne headed back out the door.

"I'm right behind you."

"That's what I'm afraid of."

"Just get goin', wise-acre." Frank pulled the door shut behind them. "Just get goin."

31

FAYETTEVILLE, NORTH CAROLINA—1967

C'MON, MASON." CARTER HOLLERED DOWN the barracks hall. "We gotta get goin'. Mush, mush. Chop chop. Get the lead out."

"Hold your horses. I'm comin' already."

"What's goin' on." Simmons staggered sleepy-eyed and hungover down the hall to see what the racket was. "Jeez, man, you gotta yell so loud, dude?"

"Of course I do. Mason is holding up the show. We have to be in Fayetteville sometime today for cryin' out loud."

"You guys are so messed up." Simmons wobbled back off to his room.

Frank came out. "I'm done."

"Thank you, your royal slowness. Now may we get the flock out of here?"

"What did Simmons want?" Frank ignored Carter's histrionics. "I thought I heard Simms."

"Forget Simmons." Carter herded Frank down the hall. "You got all your junk? We gotta split. We got a long drive today."

"Okay, okay." Frank almost dropped his small AWOL bag. He had tossed in a change of underclothes, an extra shirt, a light jacket, and a few toilet articles.

"Got shaving gear in there?"

"Ain't gonna."

"Typical. How about dough?"

"Got it."

"That's it. Let's go."

———

FAYETTEVILLE, NORTH CAROLINA WAS ONE of the least appealing GI towns Frank had ever been in. It had an unending line of bars and pawn shops out the gates of Fort Bragg. Depressing stuff. Fort Bragg itself was impressive though, at least in size. It was so big, in fact, that it had the entire Pope Air Force Base right in the middle of it.

Bragg supposedly had about 80,000 soldiers training for Nam on it, but he hardly saw any of them until they found Wayne Pike's outfit and Carter went in to drag his hometown buddy out for the weekend road trip he'd schemed up.

Wayne was training some squad, so they couldn't leave until he was done for the day and got the okay from his first sergeant. By the time he was freed up and they had got beer, food, and whatever for the trip, it was after four-thirty in the afternoon.

"What's yore name, again?" Wayne asked Frank as they started the long haul to Tennessee. He turned around in the shotgun seat and reached out his hand.

"Frank Mason." He leaned forward to shake hands.

"Nice to meet you, if I didn't already say it."

"Me, too."

"Get me a beer, somebody." Carter took one hand off the wheel.

Frank moved a couple of bags and some clothes on the seat beside him to get to a Styrofoam cooler on the opposite floorboard behind Carter that was filled with cold cans. He pulled one out, popped the top, and handed it over.

"Thanks, buddy."

"How about one for me?"

"Comin' up." Frank handed one with ice dripping down the side to Wayne. "Courtesy of Mason's Bar and Grill."

Wayne smiled. He was missing his right dog tooth. The gap made him seem a little on the crazy side.

"Show Frank how you hammer 'em down, Wayne."

"Hammer 'em down?"

"You should see this guy." Carter took a big slug of beer and set the can between his legs as he drove. "He can drink a beer faster than anybody I ever seen. Learnt it in Nam, huh, Wayne?"

"Reckon I did."

"Shoot one." Carter prompted. Wayne straightened up in the seat and squared his shoulders. "He's gettin' ready."

"You gotta prepare for it."

"Dig this, Frank."

"I'm digging." Frank didn't know what to expect.

"So what we got here, troops, is Charlie on the run." Wayne held the beer up. "We chasin' Charlie. Get Charlie. Get him now, didi mau, didi mau. Yeah!"

With a final wild whoop he leaned his head back and downed the entire can of beer and squeezed it flat with his right hand in three seconds flat.

"Aaah!" He exclaimed when he was done. "Yow!"

"Holy crap." Frank yelled. "Incredible. I never seen nothing that fast in my life. Jesus. How do you do that? I can barely even down a beer, much less slam one like that."

"It's in the squeezin'." Beer foamed at the edges of his mouth. He belched.

"One of my buddies in Goldsboro can down mugs of beer like that, but not whole cans. That was something."

"Vietnam!" Wayne whooped, turned and slapped hands with Frank.

"Lord, this is gonna be one crazy road trip."

"Another round." Carter called from the front. He tried to fast finish his beer, but mostly poured what was left down the front of his shirt. "Sonofabitch."

"Road trip, road trip." Wayne chanted. Frank got everyone another beer.

"Here's to Tennessee." He toasted, held up his can.

"And to Kentucky, don't forget. Wayne-O's got him a little woman over the gap up there."

"To Kentucky." Frank tapped beer cans with Wayne and then Carter.

"And to Fort F'in' Bragg, North by God Carolina." Wayne roared.

"Yee-ha." Frank yelled.

"Down the hatch, boys." Carter raised his can high.

He and Carter struggled to chug their beers. Wayne let go with his Nam chant and hammered his down so fast it didn't seem humanly possible.

"Get this crate up the road." He wiped his mouth with the back of his hand. "We got a long way to go and a short time to do it in. Hustle up."

"*Didi mau.*" Frank cried out. "*Didi mau.*"

Wayne swung around and slapped hands with him loudly.

"*Didi mau.*" He repeated. "*Didi mau.*"

They barreled on into the Carolina dusk, on through the Blue Ridge Mountains to the Cumberland Gap and beyond. It was all out there ahead them, all out there at the end of the concrete trail they drove. The broken white lines they sped over finally ran together, formed a long straight line like an arrow into the heart of tomorrow.

3 2

A FTER PIZZA, FRANK AND WAYNE left Margaret and the kids inside the double-wide and retired to a patio area out back of the house to drink beer and reconnect after the long gap between visits. The silence was broken only by their low conversation, an occasional voice from the trailer behind them, and the zapping of bugs straying into an electric trap hanging on a tree just beyond the patio. Margaret had herded the little ones so the "the menfolk could visit" as she explained to the disappointed kids. Frank promised to play with them the next day, and that managed to placate even Bubba, who was especially disappointed not to get to stay with his daddy and "that Mr. Mason man."

"It's a fine place you got here." Frank's words lifted softly into the quiet evening air.

Wayne lifted his ball cap and scratched behind an ear. "We're satisfied with it, I reckon."

"And a terrific family. They're a blast."

"The young'uns can be a bit tryin' now and again."

It seemed that sometimes words had to be drug out of Wayne by force. He was a man who had spent so much time working alone perhaps he'd lost some of his ability to communicate. Or maybe it was nothing more than a country person's natural reluctance to open up to outsiders, even if that outsider was someone he had known before. They went back a long way but there had been good-sized stretches where they were seldom in contact at all.

"Ever hear from Danny Carter anymore?" Frank broke the slightly awkward silence. "That was some trip we took from Fort Bragg that time, wasn't it?"

Wayne nodded slowly. "Yes, it was."

"Want another beer?" Frank opened a large Coleman cooler by his leg and pulled out a couple of cold bottles.

"Okay."

"So what about Danny?"

Wayne yawned. "Ain't heard much from him." His accent was as thick as the black Carolina night sky. "Not for quite a spell."

"Is he still around this area?"

"Naw, last I heard he was up in Virginia someplace. Got him a family. They're doin' fine, I believe."

"That's good."

There was another lull while they drank.

"Can you still hammer the brews down? Can you still chug'em in three seconds flat or whatever it was?" He got a new beer from the cooler and handed it to Wayne. "For old time's sake."

"I don't know."

"Come on."

"The old woman. . . ."

"We need to get a little buzz on here. We have some ground to cover."

"Yeah, all right."

At Frank's instigation, Wayne chugged two beers in rapid succession. If he had slowed up over the years it didn't show. Frank sipped his own, gave Wayne another to drink normally, and waited for the alcohol to work into his friend's bloodstream and loosen him up. He seemed wound too tight. Tying one on— or at least getting partly juiced—wouldn't hurt and might even help some.

"So what's it like being a tobacco farmer?"

"It's tough as hell."

"Hard to make a living?"

"Damn hard."

"The small farmer's really got it tough nowadays, don't he?"

Wayne finished his beer. "People don't know how hard it is for the small, independent farmer. You got so many things in your way. The weather, the bugs, diseases, rules and regulations, people trying to get their cut of everything you have."

"I understand that."

"Then you got your tobacco companies trying to control the market and keep the price low. The less they pay us, the less they charge the smokers, the more they sell, the better their profit margin."

"It all comes down to money. Always."

"Then there's taxes on it. And kissing the anti-smoking lobby's ass."

"I got mixed feelings about that. I want everybody to stop smoking for their own health, not because of laws and public pressure. But I hate to see small farmers go. If we could just do stuff in moderation. It's sort of like the spotted owl thing, too. If you let the timber people go, the animal goes. If the animal lives, the jobs go."

"People come first."

"That's probably what's wrong. We see only the short term. It's the long term that gets you, sooner or later. We have to take responsibility sometime."

"I suppose." Wayne turned around in his chair and looked back at the trailer. "Momma's comin'."

The trailer door opened and Margaret stuck her head out. Did all old married folk have that instinctive feel for the presence of the other? Frank wasn't sure he and the ex had ever had that. And what did it matter? Either way it was long ago. There was no use in fixating on the past—a person could easily let this living behind time crap get out of control.

Margaret stood at the door, poised either to come out or go back in. "Y'all solvin' the world's problems?"

"We'll be in directly."

"All right."

"That's a good woman you got there, bud." Frank waited until Margaret had stepped back into the house and closed the door behind her.

"She stuck with me through hard times, brother. A lot of women would've left. She's a fine mother to the children."

"I can see that."

"And she puts up with me."

"Now that's a job!" Frank joked.

"I have them moody spells. They ain't never gone away."

"You'd think they would by now. It's been over a quarter of a century."

"Hand me a beer?"

"Here you go." Frank handed over a freezing cold bottle.

Wayne opened the bottle, took a drink and set the bottle on the ground by his chair. "You know the real thing that bothers me?"

"What's that?"

"What was it all for?"

"You mean the war? I don't have a clue anymore, Wayne."

"It was about people, if you ask me. It was personal."

"You're right about that. Fifty-five, sixty thousand, whatever it was, of our dead. Maybe millions of them. That's personal. But what for? I don't know about that. I read that now we got American businesses rushing in there to get in on the Vietnamese capitalism program. We could have done that years ago and saved all the lives. They even got offshore oil rights now. That's what some people said the damned thing was fought for in the first place."

"It was about soldiers, young soldiers, dying. And killing. That's what we did."

"Yes."

"Sometimes I can still see it, feel it, smell it."

"Wouldn't it be better if you could let that go? You guys have to forget that damn war. It was a long time ago. You did the best you could. Give yourself a break. You were a young kid. What were your options?"

"I didn't go to college. It was jail or Canada."

"Exactly, exactly. But, now, buddy, it's time to wipe it clean. Saigon fell almost twenty years ago."

"It ain't easy, Frank."

"I know it ain't."

"You don't know what it was like. What we did."

"I know I don't. But I know you're a good man. Whatever it was happened to you and all the others, it happened in the past. That was another Wayne Pike, a young, inexperienced boy. Hell, that's what the military is all about. You get old guys in there and you ain't got a war. But young boys don't know. That was the young Wayne. You're the now Wayne. Forgive him and let him rest."

"It's a hard thing to do."

"All big stuff's hard."

"I reckon."

"You'll be all right. You are all right."

"I 'spose so."

"You bet. A good wife, cute kids. Heck, that Bubba's a whole family all by himself. The older boys are like Huck Finn and Tom Sawyer and Melissa's gonna be a heartbreaker."

"I reckon so."

The two men sat without speaking for several moments, slowly sipping their beers, listening to the night sounds. It was a calm, reflective time.

Wayne broke the silence. "By the way, since when does an old hippie like you, especially one that's footloose and fancy free, get to lecturin' folks on the pleasures of home life? Don't seem like you got much experience to draw on, boy."

"Maybe you're right."

"You like this here roamin' around you're doin'?" Wayne turned the conversational tables on him. "Living the swingin' single life."

"I don't think that's exactly what I'm doing."

"I'll give you this—you got a lot of guts just chuckin' everything and takin' off like you done."

"Or I'm really stupid. But it doesn't take any guts to do this kind of thing. Not really. You first just gotta be able to do it. You've got to let a lot of stuff go in your life. There's a trade off, an exchange. You have a wife, kids, a home. I have my Toyota and the road."

"Sounds like it could be all right."

"Uh-huh."

"You know where you goin'?"

"The ocean, I guess. Might as well make it a coast to coaster."

"Gonna find her." Wayne sang from the old song.

"Right."

"Where to?"

"Myrtle Beach, I suppose. I went there a couple of times back about the time we made the Tennessee trip."

"It's changed a lot."

"No doubt."

"And you come up here from the Florida panhandle?"

"That's right."

"We're way out of your way. You went the long way."

"That's okay. I wanted to see you first anyway."

"We're glad you did. The old woman thinks you're nice as can be, and the kids are all in an uproar. They think you're a celebrity or something."

"I like them, too, and Margaret's real sweet."

"Well, I ain't none too sweet, and it's way past my bedtime. We country folk turn in early."

"Turn into what?" Frank couldn't resist the obvious play on words.

"Now that's exactly why you're a damned old hippie." The two men rose to go back into the trailer. "That kind of smart-ass stuff. You'll never amount to nothin.'"

"Never will."

"Get a haircut." Wayne reached the door.

"Get a real job."

"Oh, it's a 'real' job now, is it?"

"From a rock song. George Thorogood."

"Damn hippie." Wayne closed the door behind them.

He held up a finger to his mouth to indicate they should be quiet. Margaret and the kids were already in bed.

"Damn redneck farmer." Frank retaliated in a whisper.

"I tell you, son." Wayne whispered back with a big grin. "I come by it natural, 'cause I'm just carryin' on an old family tradition. Hank Williams, Jr."

"Touché." Frank clapped Wayne on the shoulder. "Nice shot."

Wayne winked and strolled contentedly down the hall to his and Margaret's bedroom.

33

FRANK SAT ON THE EDGE of his bed and wrote in his log:

It's so southern and rural here, it reminds me of home in the 1950s a little bit. Robert E. Lee, the father of our country—Dixie's white country, of course—Jeff Davis, who no one ever seemed to care that much about, and Sherman, the devil incarnate below the Mason-Dixon.

And time here has compacted. From the 1940s to now, these areas have gone from the 19th to the edges of the 21st century. From plowing with horses to running businesses with personal computers. From squares and courthouses to Research Triangle Park. It's a hell of a cultural, societal leap. One we don't seem to be all that much happier for, either. Progress certainly hasn't made guys like Wayne any happier. But the war made him unhappy, not just progress. He never openly says it, but he believed in the war, in the cause—whatever it was.

Causes.

He paused his writing. Lately, causes had been taking a beating. The new "relationships" with Vietnam and Russia for example. Suddenly, what people believed in and fought decades for had been reversed. Flipped upside down.

Old-line Vietnamese and Russians must be taking this hard. As well as their opposite numbers here in the U.S.

And what was the lesson of it? That no belief system is worth even one person's dying for, especially when sooner or later—frequently much sooner—the reason for that dying is tossed aside as irrelevant. Self-defense, personal and national, were all you could justify. Everything else was just a bunch of temporal bull.

Oh, hell, there he went again. Mr. Pontification. Mr. On-Off. Mr. Binary. So full of it. He leaned forward to write "full of it" below his scratchings in the log but was stopped by a tentative tapping on the frame of his open bedroom door.

"Excuse me, Mr. Frank." Melissa, shy now in the less courageous light of early morning. Yesterday's midday sun had perhaps emboldened her, or maybe she was still just a little sleepy today.

"Good morning. How are you?"

"Fine."

"What can I do for you?"

"My daddy's on the telephone, and he wants to speak at you."

"Your daddy?"

"Uh-huh. He's up at Clyde's Diner. He gets coffee there most days. Are you writin' somethin'?"

Frank stood. "Yes, I am. Some notes from my trip."

"Am I—are we in there?"

"You will be." He reached down and tapped her on the nose. "You will be."

———

"THANK YOU FOR HELPING US with this grocery shopping." Margaret pushed a cart filled with picnic items—paper plates, napkins, plastic utensils, hot dog and hamburger buns. Frank walked alongside her with the kids in a mobile penumbra around him.

Nathan and Wade comprised the active part, frequently darting through the aisles and then returning to their positions, only to tear off again in roughly one minute, energy-driven intervals. Bubba and Melissa, on the other hand, were the stable part. They remained by his side, eyeing him. They walked at his pace, hung on his every word, and generally stayed close at hand.

"Not a problem." Frank bopped a happy Bubba on top of the head. Melissa tried to do the same, but Bubba pushed her hand away. "I like being with you all."

"Are you gonna stay with us, Mr. Frank?" Melissa gazed up at him.

"I need to go on down to South Carolina from here, down to the coast."

Nathan and Wade returned from their latest foray.

"Ain't you gonna go to the farmer rally? Please say you're gonna."

"Oh, yeah, I promised your daddy I would."

"Yay!"

"But, I'm probably going to leave from there."

Bubba stared at his scuffed boots. "Shoot."

"Can't you stay longer than that?" Wade shoved in next to Frank.

"You kids stop pestering Mr. Mason now. I expect he's getting tired of all your questions."

"That's all right. I don't mind, really."

"He don't mind, Momma, see?"

"Hush, Wade."

"I really need to go on. And besides, I wouldn't want to wear out my welcome with you all."

"Good heavens." Margaret exclaimed. "You wouldn't be wearing out any welcome with us. We're happy to have you."

"Thanks, but I need to finish up this cross country thing I'm on."

"Daddy wants you to stay." Melissa informed him.

"Your daddy's a good guy."

"He's so glad to see you. He needs someone to talk to sometimes. Someone other than me and the kids. Pike probably wouldn't even have gone to this rally if you hadn't come. I believe he wants to show off for you."

"Well, I wouldn't miss it for the world, then."

"Are you really from California?"

"Yes, I am, Nathan."

"My daddy says people from California are real weird."

"Nathan Pike!" Margaret rolled her eyes.

"They're just people, pal. Like anybody else. Some are weird, and some aren't. And some are *really* weird."

"Nathan, you and Wade go on and get a couple of cases of soda pop and bring 'em back here. Get mixed kinds for the children."

"Yes, Momma."

"And you, Melissa, you take Bubba and round us up four or five bags of chips. Different kinds. Not all Fritos, either. You hear me now?"

"Yes, Momma. C'mon, Bubba."

"I don't wanna."

"Momma."

"Bubba, you go on with your sister now or I'll tan your behind."

"Shoot. Dang."

"Bubba! Watch your mouth."

"All right." He let Melissa lead him away.

"They're sweet kids, Margaret. Cute as can be. That Bubba's a pistol."

"Ain't he, though. All of them sure have taken a liking to you." She pushed the cart down the aisle toward the butcher case at the back of the store.

"Goes for me, too."

The chunky, balding butcher behind the meat counter smiled at them. His full-length apron showed the signs of his trade—wet, red spots and dark stains in random disorder. The majority were collected in the area surrounding his considerable girth.

"May I help you all?"

"Thank you, anyway, sir, but I believe we'll just pick up some of the packaged meats."

"That's fine, ma'am. Be sure to let me know if you need anything."

"I will, thank you." She pointed at the meat case. "Frank, which of this hamburger do you suppose I should get?"

"Well, how much will we need? Being's how I'm something of a tightwad, I'd probably go for the less expensive, especially if there's going to be a lot of folks."

"You sound just like Pike."

"All of us old fossils are alike."

He turned away for a moment and scanned the store for the kids. Nathan and Wade were down at the end of an aisle back off to his right, but Bubba and Melissa were nowhere to be seen. When he turned back around, Margaret was dropping the last of several packages of ground beef into the shopping cart.

"You know." They moved slowly away from the meat counter. Frank pushed the cart. "I worry about Pike sometimes. I really do."

"Uh-huh?"

"He does tend to be awful blue. At odd times, too."

"A lot of fellows have had trouble getting over the war. He's one of them."

"Yes, that's true. That war was awful for some of the boys."

"I'm not around much, obviously, so I can't say for sure. You'd know better than me, but I've seen a lot worse than Wayne. I wish there was something to do. I wish we could help them. But it's something each of them has to do for himself. He has made some progress, it seems to me. I mean it seems that way, given I've only been here a little while to judge."

"No, I believe you're right, Frank. He has gotten some better over the years. One thing for sure, your bein' here has helped. He was actually in a good mood at breakfast this morning. Even if he did have a bit of a headache."

"I had a bit of one myself."

"You know he's seen a few of those VA fellows and been to some meetings with other vets. Once he went to that memorial in Washington D.C. Made him cry, he said. Now they've put up one down by the capitol in Raleigh. Not a big one like that wall or nothing, but it's something. They seem to help, but I don't know."

"Maybe they do, but I don't know, either. My personal feeling is that it would be better to let it go. Like I told him, all of the guys need to forgive themselves or whoever it is that needs forgiving and let the whole thing pass. It's time to move on."

"Mr. Frank, Mr. Frank." Melissa raced up with Bubba, their arms loaded with bags of chips. He dropped a bag of Fritos that Frank helped retrieve. When he regained control over the bags, he hugged them tightly against his Ninja Turtle T-shirt.

"What is it, Melissa?"

"Me and Bubba need to know if you want a bag of Cheetos or not?"

"No, kids. They're not exactly my favorites. But if you all want them, go ahead and get them. That is, if it's all right with your momma." The kids looked at Margaret.

"Go ahead." They jumped up and down. "Now, skedaddle. Wait—where's Nathan and Wade."

"They're up by the register." Melissa was already racing down the aisle. "They drug the pop over there."

"Regter." Bubba vainly tried to echo his sister. Frank bent down and swatted him on the backside.

"You better get your little fanny up to that 'regter."

Bubba squealed happily and tore off down the aisle after his sister, nearly dropping his bags of chips in the process.

"What a pair to draw to."

"Times two." Margaret held up four fingers. "Times two."

Frank pushed the grocery cart down the aisle toward the checkout counter. All the kids were waiting for him at the end of the aisle.

34

THE DAY OF THE INDEPENDENT farmers' rally dawned bright and clear and hot. It was one of those days where even in the relative cool of early morning the coming heat could be felt. Sweat pops out with the slightest exertion and energy drains away before the day has hardly had time to begin.

The Pike family ate a quick, light breakfast of cereal and toast, and Frank then tried to stay in the background as they hurriedly prepared for the trip to Raleigh. Nathan and Wade helped Wayne pitch a couple of large ice chests with hamburger, hot dogs, and sodas into the back of his banged up, but cleaned up, pickup. Margaret and Melissa piled grocery sacks of condiments, paper plates, plastic utensils, and snack chips beside the coolers.

Bubba—hanging onto Donatello, his favorite Ninja Turtle—and Frank supervised the packing, lending an occasional, mildly useful hand, but mostly staying out of the way. The Pikes were efficient for supposedly laid back farm folk, especially when they had a mission to accomplish. Today's was to get into Raleigh in time to join the ten o'clock parade of independent farmers around the capitol.

As far as Frank could tell from Wayne's description from the previous night, the rally and picnic after weren't expected or intended to be any big "event." It was just a gentle reminder from a nearly forgotten and essentially ignored sector of society, the small, family farmer, that they still lived in this country and that what they produced, for good or bad, was what the people of the country wanted and needed, big government and big business be damned.

Frank followed Wayne into town and in accord with the alignment created by chance and predisposition, Margaret, Melissa and Bubba rode in the Toyota with him, Nathan and Wade in the cab of the truck with their father. Spirits were high all around, and though he had prepared the Pikes for his leaving later that day, all of them acted as if he had always been in the family, as if he always would be.

Wayne's prediction about the rally turned out to be accurate. The small parade of farm trucks and tractors went virtually unnoticed, reminding Frank of a U. S. Out of Central America demonstration he'd once been part of back in Tucson. There were so few people involved it made you feel like one of the old "ban the bomb" people of the 1950s. You felt like your stand was so irrelevant to the vast majority of society that it was practically a UPG as he liked to call them—a useless personal gesture.

There were only about twenty vehicles involved, with maybe four or five tractors among them putt-putting along to provide a sense of connection to local farming. Most were just work trucks, but the families had rigged pro-small farmer banners onto the sides and hung them out windows. A couple of wiry, tobacco-chewing boys even put signs on the sides of Frank's car, hooking them to the window and door handles, thereby making him and his Toyota official participants in the parade.

The beds of the trucks were filled with enthusiastic red-faced farmer progeny who waved happily to the small clumps of people briefly gathering in front of the capitol building to stare at the motley collection of vehicles and occasionally wave back. The parade came down New Bern Avenue to the capitol, passed the Vietnam veterans memorial and the memorial for WWI, WWII and Korea, then turned down Salisbury Street, made another left on Morgan, then another on Wilmington, where they paused for a few minutes of cheering and horn honking in front of the capitol itself with its statues of the three Carolina presidents—Polk, Jackson, and Andrew Johnson.

It had been so long since Frank had been in Raleigh—he did not recall ever visiting the capitol itself before—that he felt he was experiencing it for the first time. It was as if he were a foreigner tossed up on the inland, touristy shores of this tree-filled old southern city.

Next, the parade went west out of old Raleigh down Hillsborough, then through the university area onto Western and arriving finally at Pullen Park. There they passed a large, modern glass and metal indoor swimming pool on the right and a large children's playground below the road on the left. The group parked at the top of a hill next to a large ramada. With considerable commotion, they piled out of the vehicles, the kids running off to play, the men clumped together chewing the fat, the women bustling around to get the midday meal started.

Frank observed the goings-on for a few minutes, smiling at the camaraderie among Wayne and his fellow farmers and at the industry of the country women as they patted out hamburger meat and fished drinks out of coolers for their thirsty charges. He switched his attention to the Pike children, who with a small bunch of friends played happily around the many oak and magnolia trees in the park. He was reminded of the colorful, crowded village paintings of Peter Bruegel the Elder, his favorite artist.

For a moment, the briefest of moments, seeing the group of farmers, farmers' wives, farm children, and the rest of the locals using the park filled him with a powerful sense of well being, with the fleeting sensation that everything was somehow all right after all. The world was a good place to be.

Though he was only a bystander at the outer edge of the human scene before him, still he felt for that one moment that he was a part of it, that he belonged to it, that it belonged to him. Taking a deep breath, he turned and began to walk slowly across the park grounds toward a lake he'd seen as they pulled in.

Along the edge of the water a man was helping two young boys into a paddleboat, and Frank stood in the shade of a thick oak to escape the humid Carolina heat. A trio of teenage girls went by, their bare feet crunching down the grass. He admired their wholesome, budding sensuality until the older appearing of the three saw him and gave him a haughty look.

He diverted his gaze to the sparkling lake, squinting his eyes against the bright reflection of the sun off the surface. Using his right hand to block out the glare, he saw the young boys moving fitfully about the water in their paddleboat. Behind him up the hill, a raucous volleyball game was in full swing, and beyond that several small groups of picnickers scattered around the park grounds. All in all it was a pleasing sight.

For the next half to three-quarters of an hour, he roamed the park alone, walking aimlessly, simply absorbing the sights and sounds as they came to him. He paused for a few moments while some kids played pepper with a softball and only moved on when the robust activity of the players reminded him of the inevitable eroding away by age of his own skills. Once upon a time, he hadn't been such a bad ballplayer himself.

As he climbed the hill by a double set of tennis courts, a jogger in tight, fluorescent pink running shorts whisked by. He kept track of those shorts until they dropped down below another hill and out of sight. Finally when he began to feel hungry, he concluded his meandering stroll and headed back toward the large gazebo. It was time to grab a quick bite, visit a bit more, and get out on the road again.

Back with the Pikes and their farmer friends, he got himself a beer and pulled his sweaty T-shirt away from his body as he drank. He guzzled the first, then got another to drink more slowly and walked over to where Margaret was cooking hamburgers to say his goodbyes. While he was waiting in line, the Pike children, except for Nathan, raced up red-faced and happy to the table beside him.

"Hi, kids." He patted Bubba on the head.

"Hi, Mr. Frank." They all panted at once.

"Whoa, you guys sound tired. You better get something cool to drink."

"We are, that's why we came back."

"What can I do for you, sir?" A chubby lady working beside Margaret asked.

"Well."

"I'll take care of this gentleman, Delia." Margaret told the other woman. "He's an old friend of my husband's. And I'll get my kids, too."

"All right." Delia drawled sweetly.

"Howdy, ma'am." Frank and the kids crowded round in front of Margaret.

"What can I get you? He checked out the items on the table, nearly all meat, and decided to continue to dodge that issue with the Pikes.

"I tell you what. I'm not super hungry. And I don't care for a hamburger or hot dog. So, let's see. Ah, yes, this is an old one we used to do when I wasn't too long out of the service. If you could give me a hamburger bun with mustard and relish, please."

Margaret fixed the bun and handed it to him.

"Now some of these." He picked up a pile of ridged potato chips from a plate on the table.

The Pikes watched with interest as he loaded down the bottom bun with the chips, then put the top half of the bun on top of that, and flattened out the chips with a push of the heel of his hand on the bun.

"Wow!" Bubba waved Donatello.

"A potato chip sandwich."

"Exactly, Wade. I've eaten them many a time."

"Woulda never thought of that."

Delia glanced at Margaret. "Me, neither."

He bit into the sandwich with gusto. The kids seemed to even enjoy seeing him eat. When he finished the sandwich, he had a glass of water. The children stayed around him.

"Well, guys, I reckon it's about time for me to hop in that old Toyota over yonder and take off."

"Don't leave yet." Melissa cried.

"Don't go." Bubba pointed Donatello at him.

Frank put his arm around Bubba's shoulders and with his free hand smoothed out a play-tangled curl in Melissa's hair.

"I have to, guys."

"Why do you have to?"

"That's a good question, Wade. I wish I had an answer for you. But I don't."

"Why not?"

"That's Mr. Mason's concern, Bubba. It's none of ours."

"It's all right, Margaret." He faced the three kids, but addressed Bubba. "I'm kind of on a big trip. And I'm getting near to the end. But I've got a little bit further to go, so I have to finish it up."

"You have to go now?"

"Yes, Melissa. It's something I have to do now."

"Maybe Mr. Mason will come back and see us again. You all would like that, wouldn't you?"

"Yes." The kids agreed.

"Then don't pester him so, and he probably will."

Frank winked at Margaret. "I'll be back to see you all sometime, but you're not pestering me."

He hugged Bubba and Melissa goodbye, shook hands formally with Wade, then reached across the table to shake Margaret's hand.

"No, you don't." She came out from behind the table. "I get a hug."

"Take care of yourself." He hugged her back. "And these little imps, too. Keep old Pike on the straight and narrow now."

"I will. And thanks for comin' by. It meant a lot to Pike. Please come back again. You're always welcome."

"I will."

"Promise?" Melissa and Bubba wanted to know.

"Promise."

"I hope you find what you're after."

"Thank you, for everything, Margaret."

He found Wayne in the parking lot by the gazebo, with Nathan.

"So what you up to?" He clapped Frank on the shoulder.

"Just checkin' you out. Just checkin' you out. Hi, Nathan."

"Hi, Mr. Frank."

"You got that look about you. Gettin' ready to head out?"

"Yes, I am."

"Say goodbye to the old lady?"

"And all the kids, except this one."

"Say goodbye to Mr. Mason, Nathan."

"Goodbye, sir." Nathan offered his hand.

Frank shook it in the same formal way he had Wade's just a few minutes before. "Bye, Nathan. You're a good guy. Take care of your momma and the little ones now."

"Yes, sir, I will."

Wayne tapped the boy on the shoulder. "Go on and see what they're up to." Nathan hesitated. "Go on now."

He took off across the park in a quick lope.

"Bye." Frank called to him.

"Bye." Nathan yelled back over his shoulder.

"Let me walk you to your car."

"All right."

"We didn't get a chance to talk a whole lot."

"It was a decent reintroduction, though."

"Yes it was."

"Short visits are always the best. And they set up another one for later."

"Maybe you can come back sometime after we harvest the fields. I'd have more free time then, and we could talk more seriously about things."

"I'll sure try to."

"You do that."

They reached the Toyota. "Well, old bud, thank you and your family for everything. It was fun."

"We're glad you came by."

Frank opened the driver's side and rolled the window all the way down to let some fresh hot air into the vehicle to mix with the stale hot air already accumulated inside.

"Thanks again for everything."

"Take care, brother."

They clasped hands in the old 60s style, palm to palm, with thumbs hooked and arms upright against each other. "Till next time."

"Don't take no plug nickels." Wayne lightened the farewell. "And you be sure to do everything that I wouldn't."

"You got it, buddy."

"See ya, Mason."

"See ya, Pike." Frank climbed into the Toyota and cranked up the engine.

"Purrs like a kitten."

"Just like."

Wayne stepped back and saluted.

Frank aimed his left index finger at him. "Later, dude."

Frank kept track of his friend in the rear view mirror all the way out of the parking lot and for as long as he could. Then he started searching for signs that would get him out of town and on his way south and east to where he'd been heading all along, to the coast.

35

FRANK PILOTED THE TOYOTA STRAIGHT off Highway 501 into the middle of Myrtle Beach. He vaguely recalled doing the same thing with a couple of service buddies way back when he'd been stationed up in North Carolina. But what he remembered as a small, pleasant beach town had changed drastically.

It might still be pleasant—he couldn't tell that in the ten minutes it had taken to find a parking place—but it didn't seem so small anymore. There were large hotels everywhere, and the streets were packed with vacationing middle-class Americans. The character the town once had shown had been replaced by a kind of Branson-Gone-East showiness.

Pulling out a map of the area, he stood on the sidewalk and tried to figure out where he was and what his next move would be. He had made his cross-country, coast-to-coast, ocean-to-ocean trek. Now what? What would happen now? Would this bourgeois vacation haven provide an answer to what was wrong with his life, or show him what he was to do with himself now that he was here? That didn't seem too likely.

Burying his nose in the map and forgetting for the moment the cosmic significance of having made it to Myrtle Beach, he didn't see the young woman walking up the sidewalk toward him. She had certainly noticed him and stopped beside him, standing with her left arm on her hip, one corner of her mouth turned up in a beguiling smirk.

"You lost, mister?" She gave him a head-to-toe once over. It took him several seconds to realize he'd been spoken to.

"Huh?"

"I said are you lost, mister?"

He lowered the map and regarded the girl. Except for the smooth, rich voice, the slightly ironic turn to her full lips—a turn that easily became the smirk he had missed when she first spoke to him—and a hint of maturity around her almond-round eyes, she might have been any bored college girl temporarily on the loose from her parents in this coastal tourist mecca.

"No, I'm not lost."

"Could have fooled me." She revealed fine white teeth, the front two slightly gapped.

"I haven't been here in a long time. It's changed a lot. That's the Pavilion down there past all these stores and stuff, isn't it?" He pointed behind her.

She glanced back, long enough for him to quickly take in her well-tanned legs, small waist, and round hips. He was looking at her breasts when she turned back around.

"Yes, that's the Pavilion. Been reading your tourist pamphlets I see."

"Yes, well, thanks." He folded the map and tossed it into the Toyota, then locked the door.

"Nice car."

"Hey, it got me from California to here." She began to walk away. "Uh, bye." He called after her, trying to sound conciliatory. "Thanks."

"Think nothing of it. Welcome to Myrtle Beach, Mr. California. It's the perfect tourist town." She walked away, and he again took in the dark legs, the stylish, well-filled Bermuda shorts, the sleeveless blouse.

After a moment or two, he turned and walked on down the street toward the Pavilion. He walked up and down Ocean Boulevard for the better part of a half hour before he finally rediscovered the walkway behind the Pavilion that ran alongside the strand. He took that as far as he could, then walked on the beach to Pier 14 where he settled on its patio to check out the town from a rearview, beachfront perspective.

Myrtle Beach had, indeed, changed radically over the many years. It was still beautiful, but had been heavily overdeveloped. It wouldn't be his first choice for a quality recreational experience, but it clearly was for a lot of other people. He sipped on a draft and tried to relax, leaning back in his chair, alternating his concentration between a newcomer's package he'd picked up at a visitor's center and the strolling herds of tourists on the beach.

"The geographical cure doesn't work, you know." A woman's voice broke into his reading. He slowly raised his head. It was the girl from before. "I mean, coming here isn't going to get rid of whatever you're running away from."

"Who said I'm running away from anything?"

"Don't get defensive." Her eyes sparkled mischievously.

"Then don't be offensive."

"Ooh. Snappy comeback."

He took a drink of beer.

"How about we try this again? Start over from scratch? Okay?"

"Have a seat."

She pulled a chair out across from him and sat down. Her moves were graceful and athletic and her smile so dazzling it practically made him light-headed. "Thank you."

"Would you like a beer?" He pushed the tourist pamphlet off to one side of the table. "I'm ready for another."

"Sure, thanks."

He signaled a waitress and made the order. When the beers arrived, she tried to pay, but he wouldn't let her.

"On me."

"Thank you."

She seemed less brassy now, less ironic, and more up front. She really was a pretty girl, and he was beginning to like her.

"I'm Frank Mason." He reached his hand across the table. She shook it.

"Kelly Cordel."

"Nice to meet you, Kelly."

"Likewise."

He drank down half of his beer in one long swallow. "Are you from around here?"

"Sort of."

"Sort of?"

"My folks have a condominium north of here. I came down for a few weeks before going back up to school."

"And where's school?"

"UVA, the University of Virginia."

"Want me to get you another beer?" He drained the rest of his. "While I order myself another one?"

"No. Do you drink a lot?"

"I'm sorry?"

"Do you always drink this much?"

"This is drinking a lot? These little glasses probably don't hold eight ounces. And I've only had two so far."

"I don't mean to be 'offensive' again, but that was two fast beers, I'd say."

"And?"

"Oh, nothing. It's just that drinking is a standard way of medicating feelings. The kind of thing some people do when they've been hurt or disappointed badly. Am I warm?"

"If psychobabble is your forte, maybe."

"Psychobabble, huh? But accurate psychobabble?"

"Are you a social work major at UVA, Kelly?"

"You're avoiding."

"It's a standard way of keeping your personal life to yourself."

"Do you have a place to stay tonight?"

"Excuse me?"

"Do you have a place for tonight? Did you get a room here already?"

"No and no. I was going to get a room. Why?"

"Well, I have plenty of space at my place. And the price is right."

"That's awfully nice of you, but I'm not sure."

"Are you afraid of me?"

"Not exactly."

"Well?"

"I don't know."

"I just thought I'd offer."

"I appreciate that, it's just—"

"Just what?"

"To tell the truth, I wasn't expecting anything like this. I, uh, don't know what to make of it."

"Well, it's up to you. If you'd rather stay by yourself in a motel. . . ."

He considered her for a moment and her offer. A fleeting image of El Centro and Terri flashed through his mind. She cocked her head and observed him out of the corner of her eye.

"Sure, thanks."

36

SAN DIEGO, CALIFORNIA—1992

"COME ON IN, FRANK." DAVE Holloway, his first-level GCSI manager, pointed to a chair in front of his desk.

Frank walked into the office, considered not taking a seat, then finally did. Images of Patrick McGoohan's explosive resignation in the old TV show *The Prisoner* flashed through his mind. He pictured himself standing in front of Dave's desk, banging wildly on top of it, knocking coffee cups onto the floor.

"Want a cup first?"

"Uh, no, no, I'm fine, thanks."

"Sure?"

"Sure."

"Okay, then. What can I do you for?"

He considered again what he was going to tell Dave. Maybe it was a mistake. Maybe it was a really rash thing to do. Maybe he was being immature, irresponsible. Maybe it was nothing more than another stupid midlife crisis decision. Maybe it was all that and more. Maybe he didn't give a damn.

"I've decided to resign from GCSI."

Dave shook his head like a fly had buzzed around his ears or something.

"What?" He squinted at Frank as if to bring him into better focus.

"I want to resign from GCSI."

"Whoa, Frankie." Dave got up and closed his door. "Let's go slow here."

He returned to his desk and sat back down, extending his hands, fingers locked together, across the table. Frank saw the concern, sincere it seemed, on his boss' face.

"What's wrong? Did something happen? You got a conflict with somebody?"

"No, there's no problem. No specific problem."

"Okay. I had to ask. I hope you understand."

"It was a fair question."

"Which takes us back to GCSI. I thought you were getting along fine here. You help the others. They like you. Is there some problem I'm not aware of? We can work through it, you know. That's what I'm here for."

"It's not anybody here individually. I like most everybody."

"Well, what then? Is it the assignment, somebody you work with on the technical side? These things can be changed, too. I mean, you're a grown man, you can make your own decisions, but I hate to think you might be being hasty now and regret it big time later. There are always alternative choices."

"I appreciate that, Dave, but I've decided I want to pursue other interests."

"Other interests?"

"Uh-huh."

"Like what?"

"I'm not one hundred percent sure yet. Maybe travel around. See the country a little."

"This sounds like a vacation. Why not just take one. A long one. Hell, take some extra weeks off without pay even."

"No, when I go, I'm not planning to come back. I want to do something else for a while."

"Everybody has something else they want to do. But you don't have to quit to do it."

"No, I wouldn't 'have' to quit to do it, but. . . ."

"But?"

"But I've worked for GCSI for over five years. Now I'm unencumbered personally, I've saved up some money, and I—well, I want to try something else for a while."

Dave stood up and walked back and forth several times behind the desk, apparently processing this new situation and information. Finally, he halted directly in front of Frank.

"Listen, try this on for size. How about a leave of absence? Take six months, a year off and when the leave is up, then make up your mind. I mean, you don't get paid during this time, but you keep your job and your benefits and you can start over fresh. What do you say?"

"Thanks, but I've made up my mind. It wouldn't be fair to do that. When I go, I'm gone. I'm going to resign."

"Now wait a minute." Dave sat back down behind the desk. He held up his right hand, palm out, like a traffic cop. "Let's think this over. Consider it carefully and think about the possibilities. A leave of absence, or maybe part time—twenty hours a week. Resignation is extreme. How about taking a week or so to think this over before you make a final decision?"

"Dave, I've been thinking about this for months. I don't need any more time. It's what I want to do."

"Well, hell."

"I appreciate your flexibility here. I really do."

"Then you're out of here for sure?"

"I'm gone—in four weeks if you'll let me stay on that long and get things squared away here at work. I don't want to leave you or anybody on my project hanging out."

"Then let me wish you well." Dave extended his right hand across the desk. Frank shook it. "I want to thank you, both for me and for GCSI. Now I'd like to let the rest of the crew know. Are you all right with that?"

"Yeah, sure." Frank leaned back in his chair.

He could feel the tension that had built up in him during the conversation drain away with Dave's acceptance of his resignation. It hadn't been so hard, after all.

"Give me an hour or so, and we'll announce it."

"That's cool."

Both men stood up and shook hands again. Dave walked him to the door and put one hand paternally on Frank's shoulder.

"You're absolutely sure of this?"

"Absolutely."

<h1 style="text-align:center">37</h1>

FRANK FOLLOWED KELLY'S CREAM-COLORED Jeep Wrangler up Ocean to a meticulously landscaped townhouse development on the western fringes of North Myrtle Beach. Her parents' place was on the northeastern edge of the development at the end of a quiet, dead-end street. She parked in the driveway in front of the two-car garage while he pulled the Toyota up to the curb.

Inside, he was surprised at the light, airy atmosphere created by large windows on both floors of the split level home and by a large, clear skylight dome above the second floor family room that cast a beam down onto the thick carpet. There were unobstructed views of a lushly green golf course to the north and west and of the strand and ocean from the right or east side.

A massive TV sat in one corner facing a lightweight foldout couch. Several foldout and director's chairs had been placed in front of the windows, obviously to provide maximum viewing pleasure. Along the back wall by the window overlooking the golf course was a small wet bar with several partially used liquor bottles scattered on the counter. At the far end was a replica of a five-cent peanut dispensing machine and a small microwave oven. The walls were decorated with photographic-like paintings of military fighter planes.

"Your dad a service man?" He set his bag down in front of the foldout couch.

"Uh-huh." She rustled around behind the bar for a moment to emerge with two cold beers, handing one to him. Leaning against the bar, she sipped her beer and scrutinized him, that little smirk reappearing on her appealing lips.

"Apparently he was a pilot." He sat down on the couch, his bag at his feet, the beer on a coaster atop a table in front of the couch.

"Apparently."

"Nice place you got here."

"How long were you married?"

"What? I said you had a nice place. Besides, who said I was married?"

"Why else would a man of your—uh, *maturity*—make a cross-country trek, say one all the way from California to South Carolina, unless it was to get away from a wife or an ex-wife."

"Maybe I'm just on vacation."

"Maybe the moon's made out of green cheese." She walked over to the end of the couch opposite him.

"You know, you're an extremely perceptive young woman, but you really have a fairly bad attitude."

She laughed happily. It was natural, pleasant.

"I mean it."

"No, you don't. You think I'm pretty, and you like me a lot already."

"You're pushing your luck there." He couldn't seem to get on level ground with this girl but, by God, he wasn't going to grovel. Maybe.

"Are you keeping a journal of your travels?"

"Do you have a direct line to my thoughts or am I fully transparent and don't realize it?"

"Maybe a little bit of both."

He resisted an impulse to jump up off the couch and kiss her.

"You're awfully young to pick up on all this stuff." The impulse had faded. "I suspect you're going to do well in life."

"Thank you." She walked over to the big TV, took the remote control off the top of the set, and tossed it to him.

"Here, surf to your heart's content for a minute. I'm going to order us a pizza."

As he snagged the remote, he started to say something about just having had pizza a couple of days before, but thought better of it and just powered on the set and worked through the entire dial, pausing only for a few seconds on each channel. There was something for all interests nowadays––shopping, talking, music, news, sports. Eight million channels, he exaggeratedly paraphrased Bruce Springsteen, and nothing on TV.

She pointed a phone at him from across the room. "Someday, by natural selection, channel surfing will replace sexual desire in men."

"Not this man." He paused in his own surfing when a music video came on featuring a foreign-sounding disco group fronted by an attractive blonde and an even more attractive brunette.

"So you say."

"So I say."

"You want a vegetarian pizza, right?" She punched in a number on the phone.

"Now cut that out." He squirmed on the couch.

"I take that as a yes."

"Yes, yes, take it as a damned yes."

He grabbed the remote and began surfing again. She called in the pizza order. When she was done, she brought him another beer.

"Thanks."

She settled her lithe body onto the couch near him.

"Would you like to smoke?" She surprised him yet again by producing from somewhere a thin, well-rolled joint.

"You're amazing."

"Thank you."

He wondered, vaguely hoped, he might get lucky one more time. She really was a lovely woman.

"Do you have any matches in your backpack?"

"I might." He unzipped the bag, reached into the main pocket, and drug out an old pack of waterproof camping matches. With the matches came the cross country pack of Marlboros.

"You smoke—cigarettes?"

He enjoyed the surprise in her voice for a change and didn't answer right away, setting the Marlboros on the table in front of the couch and handing her the matches.

"That really seems out of character."

"A pack-and-a-half a day for a long time, then up to two packs a day."

"It doesn't fit. I would never have guessed that. You're a middle-aged Californian. Vegetarian. Smoking doesn't go with that health conscious stratum of society."

"Well, I don't smoke anymore. But I did."

"I knew it. You tried to trick me."

"What the heck."

She wagged a finger at him and lit the joint, took a few hits and handed it over.

"Bad boy." She teased, exhaling smoke as she talked. "It's not nice to fool Mother Kelly."

"It was my only shot." He spoke between puffs. "What can I say?"

By the time they were halfway through the joint, he was loaded. When they were done, he was very stoned. He leaned back against the couch, his left shoulder almost touching her right. He could feel her warm aura, her physical being. They were both still for several minutes. From where they sat, they had a partial view of the golf course on the left, the ocean on the right. Images flickered pleasantly on the silent TV screen.

She broke the long silence. "You've come a long way to be here, haven't you?"

Her voice sounded golden, safe, non-threatening. For a moment it seemed to him that in fact he had traveled light years to arrive at this moment, but then he remembered he'd only come from Raleigh and across the country from San Diego before that.

"Not so far, I guess."

His voice sounded to him as if it came from somewhere outside his body, distant and hollow.

"Oh, I think you've come far." She put her hand on his and massaged his skin. Her touch was electric.

"You sure seem to know a lot about who I am. How is that possible? Are you clairvoyant or something?"

Her laugh sounded like music, like a song he had nearly forgotten, like a melody almost lost.

"Want me to tell you about yourself, Frank Mason? I bet I'll be close to the mark."

"Do the short version." He took her hand in his. "You're already freakin' me out as it is."

"Okay, let's see how I do."

He nodded for her to start.

"I would say, obviously, that you're divorced and that you're probably tired of your job. In fact, I suspect you hate your work. It's especially repetitive dull work, the kind that probably pays well. But fair pay or not, you feel trapped by it. How am I doing so far?"

"Fair guess, but no big revelation. The same can probably be said of sixty percent of the middle-aged men in this country."

"Then how about this? I figure the trip you're on is a quest, a personal one. You're hoping to find someone or something to anchor you to one place so you can stop running."

"Not bad. Not bad."

"Actually, you might have already seen what you were looking for but didn't realize it. Would that be possible?"

"Maybe."

"I'm sure you're also afraid that what you're doing is nothing but a symptom of a midlife crisis, but it's much more romantic to think of yourself as being 'on the road' a la Jack Kerouac. Right?"

"Don't forget Kesey and Cassaday."

He released her hand and edged away, but she moved closer to him and took his hand back in hers.

"Did I do good?"

He gazed into her intelligent brown eyes, then lower, at her lips and the small gap between her teeth. He reached his free hand up and caressed her soft cheek, then leaned forward and kissed her. She put her right hand against his shoulder. He reached his arms around her and pulled her to him. She let him kiss her once more, then pulled back.

"Let's not do this."

"Why not?"

"It might be okay but it's not what we're about."

"I didn't know we were about anything." He tried to remind himself that weed worked on him like an aphrodisiac. He needed to maintain.

She smoothed back the hair over his left temple. "I'm not trying to be prudish, and I know I've come on strong with you, but my interest was and is in you, not in going to bed with you."

"What's wrong with going to bed with me? I'm not so bad, am I?"

"Not bad at all, and I like you a lot. Under different circumstances we might have had a relationship, but this isn't the time or place. I'm not your destination or your destiny. I could be a brief encounter physically, but that would be all."

"Listen, Kelly, I'm completely amazed that you even talked to me in the first place, and your insights are right on, damn right on actually, but why does any of that preclude us from enjoying ourselves in bed."

"Sex isn't always a good thing for people to have between them, especially in a case like this."

"Oh, really. What about living for the moment. *Carpe diem.* At my back I hear time's winged chariot near. Hell, Kelly, there are only a few things a person can really have in this world. Good food, good drink, and good sex. When an opportunity like this happens and you don't act on it, it's lost. Lost forever. We don't get it back. This is the only life we know for sure we're going to have. We need to enjoy it here, now."

As if to punctuate his desperate screed, the doorbell rang.

"Damn, the stupid pizza boy."

She squeezed his hand and got up to answer the door.

"Here." Resignation was heavy in his voice as he pulled out his billfold.

"No, no, this one's on me. Or on the folks, really. Don't worry about it."

"Thanks."

She winked at him.

While she paid for the pizza, he considered his last little rant. He'd used that routine several times—it was completely sincere on his part, but it had never appealed to any of the women he'd tried it on. He wanted to be egalitarian about this gender thing, but damn it, no matter what, his experience had been that on most issues—and especially when it came to sexual relations—men and women had entirely separate agendas.

Oh, well. He let out a deep breath. There was nothing to be done about it. Sometimes you got lucky and sometimes you didn't. This time he wasn't lucky. But that sure didn't make her any less appealing or interesting.

"Here you go, travelin' man." She placed the large, hot pizza on the table before him.

"You wouldn't happen to have another doobie, would you? We could let the 'za cool and get completely ripped again."

"This is your lucky day. It just so happens that I do."

"Excellent, most excellent."

When they had done the second joint, she lifted the top on the pizza carton and took a deep breath.

"Yummie." They touched beer bottles. "To good drink and good food."

"Two out of three ain't bad." He winked at her.

"Don't forget the stuff." She pointed at the two small roaches lying in a small ashtray by the pizza carton.

"Three out of four, then. A new category."

She leaned close and kissed him on the cheek. "You'll go four for four someday—and soon."

"We'll see. We'll see."

"To whatever happens." He held a piece of pizza aloft in toast. "And whenever."

"*Salud.*" She touched a slice of pizza to his.

"*Salud.*"

38

WHEN FRANK GOT UP THE next morning after sleeping on the foldout couch in front of the TV, Kelly had already gone out. She left a note and an extra house key taped to the lid of the empty pizza carton letting him know she'd gone rollerblading and would be back later in the morning. He was to help himself to anything he wanted for breakfast and to feel free to use the bathroom to clean up.

Shaking beer and weed cobwebs out of his head, he did just that. He took a long, warm shower and then ate two slices of perfectly-browned toast which he sweetened with a little raw honey he found in a corner of the well-stocked refrigerator. By nine-thirty he was ready to go.

The only problem—go *where?* Do what?

He had made his cross-country trip. He'd done what he guessed he'd set out to do in the first place—put as much distance between himself and his recent past as he could. Myrtle Beach was a long way from San Diego. On the journey he'd met some interesting people and reconnected with family and a lot of old friends. That wasn't bad. Even if he hadn't come to any grand conclusions about his life or figured out what he wanted to do with the rest of it, the traveling had been worthwhile.

He was still breathing wasn't he? That was the main thing. Stay in this thing, whatever it is, as long as you can. He remembered a bumper sticker he'd seen once that said "The one with the most toys at the end wins." Funny, but not true. The one who stays around the longest with the most faculties intact, that's who wins.

Putting his thoughts on hold for a few moments, he packed his bag and found pencil and paper to leave a goodbye note. He thanked Kelly for her hospitality and her weed and told her how much he enjoyed their conversation and how perceptive she was, despite a decided list toward New Age psychobabble. He figured she might find that comment mildly humorous.

Cranking up the Toyota and puttering through the quiet development, he was surprised at how easily he found his way out. He headed back into Myrtle Beach on Ocean Boulevard and considered his present position in the scheme of things.

Yeah, he was getting older. And, yeah, he was going to die. Sooner than he would ever want it to come. But he wasn't dead yet. Death ended it all. Big deal. Death robbed life of all meaning. Big deal. He wasn't dead yet. He was still alive. He could still hope. He could still try to make something out of what time he had left. He had seen and experienced quite a few things on his coast-to-coaster. Maybe he'd seen enough now, maybe it was time to do something.

He glanced over at the ocean, glistening under the bright but not yet hot rays of the sun. Seabirds, gulls of some kind, glided easily over the placid surface of the water. Occasionally one would drop, diving for food. He admired their graceful movements, their practical beauty.

Inhaling a deep breath of the wet, saline air, he slowly released it. Without warning, an unexpected wave of optimism flooded over him. There was time yet, maybe not as much as he would want, but perhaps enough. Enough time to begin again, to start over, to make another life.

Then, unbidden, the memory of Memphis and Kim flashed once more in his mind. He saw her standing in front of the hotel counter, laughing in the blues bar, waving goodbye. Maybe he should go back to Memphis. Back to Kim. If her offer was still on. There were never guarantees, anyway. They might not last any longer than up to her next big assignment or transfer or his next need to hit the road—how could you know?

He was certain he'd learned one thing from life, however. Nothing lasted forever. Nothing. It wasn't supposed to. And he had learned that you should never expect too much from life, be prepared for delayed gratification. Man, he felt he knew about that. Sometimes he thought his whole damn life was one long exercise in delayed gratification.

He also knew that at his age the possibilities for gratification were becoming fewer and fewer with each passing day. There seemed to be so little you got in this life and none of it you could keep. The best you could hope for were occasional, fleeting moments of contentment—he hesitated even to think of using a word like happiness. That would be too much to expect.

He also knew perfectly well that everyone was on borrowed time. And the bill might come due when we least expected or were prepared for it. Yet as long as we were breathing, there was the promise of another tomorrow. And what that tomorrow might be like was always worth finding out.

With each new day you could start over, see where you were, where you'd been, where you might go. And you could adjust your attitude. He knew his wasn't much of a philosophy and that it was austere, but he could live with it.

If things didn't work out with Kim or whomever it might be if it wasn't to be her, well, so what? He still had some savings left. He still had the Toyota. He had some time remaining. He had his life yet. Granted that didn't necessarily seem like a lot, but it beat the hell out of the alternative.

Out on Business 17, he pulled into a service station to gas up and check the oil and tires. He bought a bottle of grape juice and a small pack of cashews for the road. The clerk took his money.

"You come a long ways?"

"How's that?"

"Lots of folks here have come from far away."

"California." He collected his change.

"That's far away, all right."

"Yes it is. It's far away."

Back in the Toyota, he rummaged in his pack and found the Marlboros that had accompanied him since El Centro. El Centro—that seemed so long ago, or was it just yesterday? He opened the box. There were three cigarettes left. He had never smoked a single one. He started the Toyota and drove up to a dumpster sitting square, ugly, and dirty brown at the back of the station lot.

Crumpling up the box, he reached out the rolled down window and tossed the pack into the dumpster.

"It's easy to start over. All you gotta do is throw away everything you ever had before and begin again. Easy."

He pulled out into the traffic. Yes, it would be a new beginning, a new start. Easy or not. That's all you could hope for or expect—any way, any time. As he drove out of Myrtle Beach it occurred to him that with all things considered, at least for the time being he was okay with where he was.

He wasn't much concerned about the past, and he'd let tomorrow take care of itself. When he reached the highway, he hit the gas and sped on back toward the west. As he rolled along, windows down and fresh air blowing in his face, he was in good spirits. He felt pretty darned good.

J.B. HOGAN IS A PROLIFIC and award-winning author. He grew up in Fayetteville, Arkansas, but moved to Southern California in 1961 before entering the U. S. Air Force in 1964. After the military, he went back to college, receiving a Ph.D. in English from Arizona State University in 1979.

J.B. has published over 250 stories and poems. His novels, *The Apostate, Tin Hollow, Time and Time Again: The Curious Case of Mr. Stephen White, Losing Cotton,* and *Mexican Skies*—as well as his local baseball history book, *Angels in the Ozarks,* a short story collection entitled *Fallen,* and his book of poetry, *The Rubicon*—are available at Amazon, iBooks, Barnes & Noble, Books-A-Million, and Walmart.

When he's not writing or teaching, J.B. plays upright bass in East of Zion, a family band specializing in bluegrass-flavored Americana music, and is active in the Washington County (AR) Historical Society, where he's recently served as President.

www.thejbhogan.com